COMING HOME TO DREAM VALLEY

S J CRABB

Copyright © S J Crabb 2021

S J Crabb has asserted her rights under the Copyright, Designs and Patents Act 1988 to be identified as the Author of this work.

This book is a work of fiction and except in the case of historical fact, any resemblance to actual persons, living or dead, is purely coincidental.

All rights reserved. No part of this book may be reproduced or transmitted in any form without written permission of the author, except by a reviewer who may quote brief passages for review purposes only.

NB: This book uses UK spelling.

ALSO BY S J CRABB

The Diary of Madison Brown
My Perfect Life at Cornish Cottage
My Christmas Boyfriend
Jetsetters
More from Life
A Special Kind of Advent
Fooling in love
Will You
Holly Island
Aunt Daisy's Letter
The Wedding at the Castle of Dreams
My Christmas Romance
Escape to Happy Ever After
Cruising in Love
Coming Home to Dream Valley
Christmas in Dream Valley
sjcrabb.com

COMING HOME TO DREAM VALLEY

When Sammy Jo heads to Dream Valley to marry eligible bachelor Marcus Hudson, on the surface, it appears she has everything.

Previously unlucky in love and desperate for a new beginning, she is hopeful for a gorgeous new life.

But this is no ordinary match made in heaven and when Sammy learns the reason behind the proposal, she has a very difficult decision to make.

If she marries the man she loves, she could destroy Dream Valley and if she walks away, it will be nursing a broken heart.

Curl up with a sweet, cosy romance with a little twist to brighten your day and discover an array of quirky characters in a place where magic happens and dreams come true.

PROLOGUE

The car reaches the top of the hill and we both sigh with delight.

"Wow, Jake wasn't kidding, this place is amazing."

Florrie sounds as excited as I feel as she looks forward to meeting the man who has changed her life so dramatically.

Stretching before us like the finest watercolour painting is a land that received every one of nature's blessings. Green undulating hills stretch for miles against the backdrop of a sparkling sea. Little tiny buildings nestle inside valleys and the sun is bright as it lightens our spirits and provides warmth for the livestock who graze in the lush fields. Wild flowers line the grassy banks and as new homes go, this one is the finest.

"I can't believe we're finally here. It's amazing."

I am also eagerly anticipating the place that will change my life forever and say slightly nervously. "Is it far?"

She squints at the Sat Nav. "Four miles, not long now."

We pass a sign welcoming us to Dream Valley and I think back on how much my life has changed since the cruise.

That final week was the most amazing week of my life. I

spent most of it with Marcus, who, quite frankly, took my breath away. He was intriguing, attentive and the perfect companion and a delicious shiver passes through me when I think we'll be reunited in less than thirty minutes.

Florrie is wrapped up in her own thoughts and I sigh, "I feel a little envious."

"I'm sure you do." I know my friend thinks I'm mad and who can blame her when you think about the reason I'm here at all? Today we are heading to Valley House. The home of the Hudson brothers and their mother, Camilla Hudson. We are about to meet my future mother-in-law and perhaps Florrie's in the future if things work out with Jake.

"Do you think it will be ok?"

She throws me a sympathetic look. "I'm sure of it. How do you feel about meeting Marcus again? Do you feel nervous at all?"

"I'm looking forward to it." I shrug. "If anything, I'm worried about what his mother will think. Do you think she knows about our, um, arrangement?"

"Jake says no and we're not to say anything. One thing I've learned is the guys dote on their mother and want her to be happy."

"Yes, Marcus told me that in her company we must appear like any newly engaged couple planning a wedding."

"And you're still ok with that?"

"I am. You see, Marcus is perfect for me, he just needs to work that out for himself."

"You do know you can back out; you don't have to go through with it."

"Coming from the bride who jilted her groom at the altar."

"With very good reason."

I laugh. "Did you manage to catch up with him when you returned? I never asked."

Since we returned, I've hardly seen Florrie. We've both been busy sorting our lives out and tying up any loose ends, ready for our move to Dream Valley.

"Yes, I called him, and we met at the Red Robin for lunch one day."

"Did he bring *her*?"

"No, thankfully. Apparently, she thought it was best we met alone, to settle the past and move on."

"She was probably worried you'd slap her. I know I would."

She laughs out loud. "What, slap the woman who did me a huge favour? I'd probably hug her instead and swap friendship bracelets or something."

I laugh just thinking of it. "So how was it? Did it feel strange seeing him again?"

"It did. The thing that struck me the most was how much of a stranger he was. It had only been a little over two weeks and yet when I saw him, it was as if we were old acquaintances and nothing more."

"That's good then."

"Yes, maybe it's because it felt as if I had been away for months because so much happened. When we returned, home seemed different somehow and made my decision easier."

"Did you tell him?"

"Yes. I told him I was making a fresh start and moving on. He was surprised but seemed happy for me, probably because he won't have to face me in the street and see me around town."

"So how did you leave things?"

"I handed the ring back, at his request."

I can't believe what I'm hearing. "Wow, he really asked for that back. I would have told him I tossed it in the sea in a fit of rage."

"The thought did cross my mind, but then again, I don't really want any reminder of him, anyway. No doubt he'll sell it to buy his new wife a car or something."

"Was it that expensive? I never knew."

"I think so. He told me it cost him three months' salary, and he was on a good wage."

"Then I would definitely have kept it as payment for the emotional trauma he put me through."

My own rings sparkles as I grip the wheel and I sigh. As decisions go, this one has to be up there with the worst ones I've ever made because it's purely based on wishing for a miracle, which is that Marcus will fall desperately in love with me and realise he can't live without me. Then again, it would be a miracle because the tales Jake has told Florrie about his brother don't make for happy listening.

I say with interest. "So, did you tell him about Jake? I would have loved to see the look on his face when you told him you had met someone already."

"I didn't. The less he knows about me, the better. I never want to see him again and he doesn't have the right to know my plans."

"Good for you."

"Do you know, he even wanted me to write a note to all the guests to apologise and give him half the money for everything he paid out for, which wasn't much because my parents paid for most of it."

"You were right to jilt him, Florrie; you deserve better."

She nods in agreement. "You can say that again."

"So, how did it end?"

"I gave him the ring back and told him I was glad I was leaving and would never have to see him again. He just shook his head sadly and said it was for the best, and he was happier now than he'd ever been. Honestly, the man is a monster. He was so patronising, telling me I may be angry now, but one day I would meet someone and know it was the right thing to do. He even told me not to cling on to the memory of him because it would hold me back from finding anyone else."

I roll my eyes. "It's his new wife I feel sorry for. She's stuck with the creep. What did your parents say when you told them about Jake?"

There's an awkward silence, and I say incredulously, "You did tell them about him, didn't you?"

"No." She exhales sharply. "How could I tell them I'd already met someone so quickly? All I said was I'd accepted a job and was moving in with you. I told them I needed a fresh start, and they were happy for me. I'll fill in the details when I've had time to settle down and see where this is going with Jake. Do you think I did the right thing?"

She looks anxious because I know she hates lying to her parents, and I say firmly, "They will only want you to be happy. I'm sure that when they see you together, it will put their minds at rest. You know, we are luckier than most because we have an exciting future ahead of us. I just hope it all works out and Dream Valley really is the promised land."

As we pass through some large gates, telling us we have reached Valley House, I stare at the future with my eyes wide open. Have I made the right decision?

I'm counting on it.

As we drive towards our future, I'm full of hope for what lies ahead of us, and Dream Valley and the Hudson brothers could be the pot of gold at the end of two extremely long overdue rainbows.

CHAPTER 1

Just seeing Marcus waiting for me reminds me why I agreed to this crazy scheme in the first place. I must have doubted my sanity a million times already since I met him on the cruising in love programme.

The fact I've always been a disaster where it concerns men should have told me I was in permanent leave of my senses because I just shouldn't be allowed out–ever. Now I've agreed to something so foolish I can't even admit it to myself and as the engagement ring flashes in the sunlight, I swallow hard when I see the welcoming committee.

Florrie is so excited beside me as she spies Jake her own success story and my heart sinks because why did everything fall into place for her with no conditions attached?

She left one bridegroom at the altar and met another before her honeymoon was even over and I should know because I was on that honeymoon in place of the groom.

Jake will be good for Florrie because he is just what she needs. Fun loving, easy to be around and full of wicked jokes and a view of life many would envy. It was just my luck to fall for the dark, brooding, complicated brother of her new boyfriend, who is the total opposite of him.

Then there's me, the enthusiastic bridesmaid who thought dating seven men at sea would be fun, only to fall for someone completely different who sees me as a business opportunity and nothing else.

Not to forget their other brother, Dom, who was also keen to involve me in his own crazy scheme, and I'm slightly worried that I have 'gullible' tattooed on my forehead because I obviously attract the weird ones.

As we pull up, the gravel flies and I swear I see his mother duck and worry that we sent a stone rocketing to her head. Not a good first impression to your soon to be mother-in-law because, like an idiot, I agreed to marry a man for business purposes only. However, she must never find out because they have just lost their father, and this is all a result of his last will and testament.

Florrie says with excitement, "Oh my goodness, we're here. I can't believe it and I'm struggling to breathe. Jake looks amazing. I forgot how handsome he is. How lucky am I?"

I nod. "Yes, um, we both are."

She looks at me sharply because she knows all too well what the real score is and says softly, "You know, you can still back out. Tell Marcus you've changed your mind and blame it on the sea air or something in the water."

"What, a curse from Neptune from the depths of the ocean, or the truth that I'm the only gullible fool on the cruise ship who was sucked in and made the craziest decision of her life?"

She shakes her head. "I'm guessing you thought of that already and decided to go with it. You know, Sammy, you really don't have to honour every commitment you make.

Sometimes you can say no. You won't be struck by lightning if for once you do the right thing for you."

"How can I, just look at him?"

We both look at my fiancé by default, and I must admit he is one in a million. Dark hair with dark flashing eyes that make you forget every principle you own when he looks in your direction with an intensity that strips every rational thought from your mind. Then there's the physique crafted in perfection by his strict fitness regime and an attitude of control that scrambles a girl's mind.

He hooked me on his line and reeled me in, and I didn't even put up a fight. I went there willingly because if I have one goal in life right now, it's making this fake engagement a marriage made in heaven and deliver a happily ever after that's long overdue.

As the engine stops, I prepare for the biggest mistake of my life as the door flies open and I am pulled from the car by a very ferocious woman.

"Oh, my darling, let me look at you."

She pulls back and checks me over and I feel slightly uncomfortable as she sizes me up so publicly.

"Hmm, you look a little pale, my dear and could possibly use some iron tablets and a few multi-vitamins. I think I have some in the kitchen you could use. Trust me, they make all the difference."

I'm at a loss for what to say as a strong hand slides around my waist and pulls me close to a body I have been dreaming of since he left me on the dock at Fort Lauderdale.

"Sammy, I've missed you."

I'm speechless as he pulls me into his arms and before I know what's happening, he leans in for the most passionate kiss of my life so far.

I'm actually loving life right now as he kisses me hard and with a passion I'm keen to explore further.

I hear a disgruntled, "For goodness' sake," and look up to see his brother Dom watching the spectacle angrily. I wonder if the kiss was more for his benefit than to present the perfect image of the happy couple to his mother, who is watching the scene with a misty expression.

Luckily, Jake saves the day and sweeps Florrie into his arms and spins her around, before dipping her to the floor in one spectacular romantic gesture and her laughter makes me smile because theirs is a genuine connection that I'm keen to see develop.

"Jake, oh my goodness, put Florence down. What will the neighbours say?"

"We don't have any neighbours in case you've forgotten."

Marcus grins as Jake rolls his eyes and their mother shrugs. Then Dom says angrily, "Not yet, anyway, but if Marcus gets his way, we could have them surrounding us before the year is up."

An awkward silence descends on the welcoming committee, and his mother looks confused.

"Surely not, darling. Marcus wouldn't want strangers in our midst. No, we need to preserve our privacy at all costs. I mean, it's bad enough having public footpaths littering the estate and just don't get me started on that, or none of us will enjoy the lovely spread I have prepared to welcome the new additions to our growing family."

I hear Jake whisper loudly, "You mean that Waitrose provided. The only thing mum did was place the order online."

"What was that, Jake?"

Camilla looks interested. "Did you say my delivery has arrived? You know, Amazon Prime is surely a miracle from God. I only ordered the foot spa yesterday and I've already had a message from dearest Alexis that it's on its way with Roberto, the super-efficient delivery driver."

I stifle a giggle at the impatient look on Marcus's face as he growls, "Alexa mum, for the millionth time you say Alexa and might I just remind you, she is not a real person."

"Nonsense dear. We have some lovely chats over coffee and cake. She knows a lot and has recommended so many recipes to me I'm thinking of starting my own YouTube channel, or what's that other thing everyone's raging about now, toktikkety?"

I glance at Florrie who is struggling to breathe as Marcus growls. "For gods' sake, I give up. Come on, darling, I'll show you around."

"Remember my sumptuous feast, darling, don't go rekindling your passion before you've sampled my delicious horsdoevres."

Marcus grabs my hand and pulls me quickly from the crowd, and I struggle to keep up with him. In fact, I wish he would slow down because, quite frankly, his home takes my breath away. Manicured lawns, roses trail just about everywhere amid a historical stone-washed building that looks as if it's lived a thousand generations. I can't even begin to imagine what living here must be like, and I pinch myself that I'm here at all.

Marcus promised that Florrie and I can share a new apartment in town, but for now I'm keen to soak up the atmosphere and explore this amazing piece of history.

However, he has other ideas and pulls me through a large oak door into a beautiful wood panelled hallway and slams it with a resounding thud.

"I'm sorry, Sammy. I tried to talk her out of the welcoming committee and intended on plying you with enough alcohol to help you with the shock of meeting her for the first time."

"She seems lovely. You shouldn't be worried."

"No, Sammy, I should be very worried because the more

time you spend with her, the sooner you'll lose your own mind. Just take what she says lightly and do what you want because my mother is a force of nature that needs to be survived, not admired."

I feel surprised that he speaks of her this way because on the cruise it was evident how much they all dote on Camilla Hudson. A woman that must be protected from harsh reality at all costs it seems, because she can't suspect a moment of our fake engagement and I suppose that was the reason for the passionate welcome.

As I follow him, my lips still burn from the searing kiss he delivered, and my head is still scrambled with how that made me feel.

He may have been pretending, but I certainly wasn't and now I'm keen to play my part well because if I can't make this man crafted from my dreams fall in love with me, then I will have failed at life.

As I follow him to God only knows where, I decide to fashion myself into his perfect woman at all costs and I don't care if that makes me look a desperate fool because I am. He will just think I'm playing my part well, which makes it a win-win situation. At least I hope it will be.

CHAPTER 2

I'm completely speechless. I have ended up in Marcus's bedroom, of all things, and can't even look at the huge king-sized bed dominating the room. It feels wrong to be here at all, and I wonder why he brought me here first. It feels a little weird if I'm honest and I say slightly nervously, "This is lovely, um, do you have any further training in mind?"

The only reason I can think of is that Marcus has recruited me twice over, once as his fiancée and once as his house demonstrator for his property empire. On the cruise, both Florrie and I were trained in his cabin on how to present a house and so that must be why he brought me here.

He shakes his head and says bluntly, "No, I thought you'd like to settle in first, maybe freshen up and prepare yourself for the ordeal of a lifetime, otherwise known as the welcome brunch party."

I feel slightly touched but could have coped and say lightly, "Oh it's fine. My stuffs in the car, anyway and I can freshen up when I reach the apartment you arranged."

Something about the look in his eyes tells me I'm not

going to like this, and he says slightly guiltily, "Um, about that…"

"What?"

"I'm afraid the builders are a little behind. I did wonder if they would slacken off when I wasn't here to project manage them and it appears I was right."

"So, we have nowhere to stay."

I look at him in horror and for the first time since I met him, he looks a little uncomfortable.

"You do and you're looking at it."

"Here!"

He shrugs. "Mum said she didn't mind you and Florrie staying at Valley House. She, um, told Jake and me that she was a modern woman and didn't mind that sort of thing as long as we're careful."

I almost want to laugh at the tortured expression in his eyes and for some reason, it reveals a sliver of humanity inside the normally guarded, cold-hearted man I appear to have developed a taste for.

"But how?"

I look at the huge bed with a mixture of excitement and dread, and he shrugs.

"It's big enough. We can make a barrier if you like, or I could sleep on the floor."

"You would do that?"

He sighs heavily and nods. "If it makes you feel more comfortable."

"Or I could share with Florrie, and you could share with your brother."

He looks a little disappointed, and it feels good seeing some emotion in a normally controlled person.

"If they agree. I'm guessing neither of them would be happy about that because Jake can't stop talking about Florence."

Thinking of my friend and how much she has been looking forward to seeing him again, I already know she will be more than happy about our new sleeping arrangements.

I suppose I'll just have to trust him to be a man of honour, and so I sigh and smile weakly.

"Ok, fine, I'm sure we can make this work."

He nods and turns away before I can register any kind of emotion in his eyes and says abruptly, "Anyway, if you give me your keys, I'll bring your cases up. I've cleared you a space in my wardrobe and the top two drawers in the chest in the bathroom. Make yourself at home and don't worry, I'll keep out of your space as much as I can despite the fact we're engaged and meant to be crazy about one another."

As he heads off, I'm left feeling conflicted. Part of me wants to cry and part of me is jumping for joy. This is an unexpected plot twist I never saw coming because if I want to make Marcus fall in love with me, surely this is the perfect opportunity.

Wandering around his bedroom feels wrong on every level.

It's as if I'm invading his soul because he is everywhere. From the dark masculine furniture and charcoal walls to the silver silk sheets on the bed and the brass light fittings. Even the art is angry in this room, a swirl of dark stormy colours in some form of abstract nightmare.

For some reason, Marcus Hudson lives a troubled life because there isn't anything here to tell me otherwise.

I walk into his ensuite bathroom and feel relieved to see a bath and separate shower. It appears this family wants for nothing because every modern convenience is in sight. Gleaming enamel and polished chrome, mixes with charcoal fluffy towels and strong masculine toiletries that crowd the shelves behind the huge mirror above the sink.

It feels wrong to even open the cupboard and delve into

his personal space, but I can't resist unscrewing the cap on his aftershave and letting it waft through my senses.

I'm not sure when I fell in lust with Marcus Hudson, probably as soon as I met him on the cruise ship, but it turned out to be a dance with the devil because it doesn't seem to be reciprocated.

He wants me for one thing only and that's my signature on the marriage licence, so he can claim his inheritance and develop Dream Valley into his version of Utopia. Definitely against his brother's wishes, perhaps his mother's and I wonder what will happen if he gets his own wish and carries out the threat.

I think about his brother Dom, who tried to attract me in a different way entirely. He tried to date me and make me fall in love with him, to sprint past Marcus to the altar and lay claim to the inheritance himself. He looked angry when we arrived and stormed off rather than watch this farce unfold and I wouldn't put it past him to steal it at the last minute by producing a mail-order bride from thin air.

Sighing, I look out of the window and see Marcus heaving my cases out of the car, and I take a moment to enjoy the view. He is so impressive. It hurts just thinking about the moment when this arrangement ends and I'm packing them away again. Tall with dark hair and stormy eyes, he looks as if the world angers him on repeat. Broad shoulders are the result of a fitness regime an athlete would be proud of, and his clothes hang off his body as if they can't bear to let go. Even his shirts cling to him like a desperate lover and my heart quickens at the thought of a man like that beside me at night.

Can I see this through without revealing the lust I have for this man? I can pretend with the best of them, but what happens if I forget behind closed doors? It's almost certain I'm in for a rough ride of my emotions and in danger of losing my mind, but I must try to cleanse him from my heart, hoping that the reality definitely doesn't live up to the dream.

I want to end up needing to walk away, grateful that I can at least and so part of me is hoping Marcus Hudson turns to be everything I hate in life, instead of all my dreams come true.

CHAPTER 3

By the time he returns, carrying my case effortlessly, I think I've unscrambled my head and as he enters the room, I say lightly, "So, what's the plan?"

Dropping the cases onto the floor, he rakes his hand through his hair and shrugs. "We play the happy couple in public and friends in private. You know, Sammy…"

He looks at me with admiration and I like how that makes me feel. "I really am grateful for this. I know it's asking a lot and I don't deserve it, but I want you to know I'll make it extremely worth your while."

"I know. It's fine, I needed a fresh start, anyway."

I make light of it because it's true at least. I do need a new start because being jobless meant I'd soon be homeless, and this came at the perfect time for me. A shot at doing something adventurous—and with him as added candy to the pack. I would have been a fool to refuse.

"Will I be starting work tomorrow?"

I'm curious about the job as his property assistant, and he nods. "Yes, I'll take you to the office I rented in the nearby town. I say town…" he shakes his head. "More like a village, but it gets me away from this madhouse and enables me to maintain some kind of professionalism. We have a lot to arrange, what with the wedding itself and then the subsequent handling of the will."

Sitting on the bed, I look at him thoughtfully. "When we discussed this on the cruise, you said we had to stay married for two years. Will it take that long to receive your inheritance? How will that work?"

He shakes his head and leans against the wall, and I swear to God my soul shivers as I play out every dirty thought in my head right now.

"No, all we need is the licence, and then we present it to the solicitor, and he starts the paperwork to sign this property over to me. There's a codicil in it that if we divorce inside two years, the property reverts to the estate. Any changes during that time go with it, so we can at least start applying for the planning permission I need to start creating a town anybody would be proud to live in."

Suddenly, he smiles, and I catch my breath because it completely transforms him. He looks excited, more approachable even, and I stare at him with a hunger I struggle to contain. I am fan-girling over a man who doesn't even notice my infatuation, which is a huge blow to my ego because I never had a problem attracting men before. Not him though, he's so different from the usual men I meet, and he straightens up and says with excitement. "I'll show you the plans tomorrow, I think you'll like them."

"And your brothers, your mum?"

He shrugs as if he couldn't care less what they think, which worries me.

"They'll soon come round and see it's the best thing for all of us. The Hudson family has kept hold of this place for generations and now it's time to create something that will earn them their place in history. Why should so few people have such riches when we can create a little piece of paradise for everyone to enjoy? I have the planning department hot for this because they get to realise their goals and provide homes for the locals without having to search for land."

He smiles at me with an excitement that's infectious and says with excitement, "You have agreed to make history with me, and I will never forget that."

Holding out his hand, he says gently, "Come on, mum will be dying to get to know you and we need to start our campaign."

As my hand closes around his, I feel a delicious thrill pass through me as I sense destiny stepping aside as we push through the door. Two years to make all my dreams come true on the back of his. How hard can it be?

WE JOIN the rest and once again I'm blown away by the sheer opulence of the Hudson mansion. As places to stay go, it's more like a five-star hotel because I have never seen such luxury.

Catching sight of my friend, I don't miss the sparkle in her eyes or the flush to her cheeks as she laughs at something Jake whispers in her ear, and I feel happy for her. Florrie deserves happiness after discovering her bridegroom was already married when she went to join him at the altar. Shocks like that aren't easy to recover from, and yet Jake has made the impossible happen. He has taken her hand and led her down a different path, and I'm happy for them both. I wish I had that same reassurance, although the fact that Marcus' hand is currently wrapped around mine certainly makes it look that way.

His mother's eyes shine as she sees us coming and says happily, "Here you are. Come in, Sammy, and let me hear everything about you. I'm dying for some female conversation around here and now I have two lovely ladies to spoil and get to know.

It's almost impossible not to love everything about Camilla Hudson. From her slightly crazy dark hair that escapes its messy bun, almost as if she was in a hurry to restrain it, to her sparkling brown eyes that are so like her sons and the smile she wears so well chases away any doubts I had of coming here.

As Marcus pours the champagne, I head to her side, and she smiles. "So, we have a lot to organise in a very short space of time. You must share your bridal Pinboard with me. I can cast my eye over it and make it happen if you like."

"My what?" I feel as if I've failed at the first hurdle already, as she grins and cocks her head to one side. "Pinterest, darling. I swear by it. I have it all worked out already if it helps. One wedding for each of my sons with ideas galore. I also have a baby shower board, a hen party one and the dream home I imagine for each of them. There are also ones on amazing honeymoons that I'm sure will tempt you, so if you like we'll compare boards and see if we have a match."

My mind is buzzing as Florrie looks on with interest. "Wow, I would love to see your boards; can I share too?"

"Of course, my dear, I have one for Jake, Dom and Brad. Marcus is the first to need it though, so we may as well start with him."

"Honestly, mum, Sammy doesn't want to think about all that now, give her some space?"

Marcus hands me a glass of champagne and shakes his head, looking a little worried which makes my heart sink. He hates this, every minute of it, and it's obviously because he doesn't think of me that way. I'm guessing he would prefer a quick trip to the registry office, followed by a meal out for the family before heading back to the office.

Just imagining how amazing Camilla's board must be makes me curious and I say defiantly, "I would love to swap boards, but must confess I haven't had time to start mine yet. Maybe I can take inspiration from yours."

Camilla looks shocked. "What, no Pinterest board mapping out your life? Goodness, I need to educate you. Every woman needs a plan, darling and something to aspire to. I'll be happy to help you set one up and send you pins you may be interested in."

She shakes her head as if she's facing an alien in her own home and I don't miss the look she shares with Florrie, who I know has a similar outlook on life. When she was planning her own wedding, it was run like a military operation, and she had every I dotted along with every T.

Florrie comes to my rescue and says quickly, "I suppose Sammy was so busy helping me with mine, she forgot to set one up for herself. Never mind, we can work on it together."

Marcus exhales sharply. "Leave her alone, mum. Sammy will organise everything just the way she wants—how *we* want it, and you just need to show up."

He looks irritated and I don't miss that the light dims a little in Camilla's eyes and I rise to her defence. "Actually, Camilla, I would love your help. Welcome it even."

Staring pointedly at her son, I'm surprised to see a little burst of approval from his eyes as he holds me captive with a stare that will never stop making me lust after him. In fact, I feel a little heated just being the focus of his attention because when he wants to be, Marcus can hold your attention as if there is no one else in the room. Just the way he runs his fingers through his hair and looks slightly out of his comfort zone makes me want to run to his side and reassure him that everything will be alright.

Hating the hold he has over me, I drop my eyes from his and fix Camilla with a beaming smile.

"Maybe we could start now…"

"Sammy!"

Marcus's voice holds a warning, and I look at him in surprise. "We have other things to do this afternoon, you won't have time."

Camilla exhales and shakes her head. "Then we will have to schedule it in tomorrow some time."

Fixing me with a smile, she laughs softly. "It's fine. Marcus has been longing for your arrival almost as soon as he returned home. The preparations can wait a day or two while you catch up."

Marcus nods and I wish it really was the case, but knowing him it's business all the way, so I smile politely and look at Florrie for some courage and hate the pity in her eyes as she reaches for her glass.

The food that Waitrose has prepared is very welcome and as we sit and chat, I notice that Dom never made it to the celebrations, and I feel bad about that. I know they were in a competition to win my hand on the cruise and I should have chosen him. At least he pretended to fancy me, to want to be with me, but Marcus was straight from the start. This is a business arrangement and nothing more, so I should be grateful for that, at least.

If Dom had got his way, I would have fallen for his charms and tossed my heart out there to be broken.

Trying not to dwell on the fact it may already be too late for that, I resign myself to the situation and just stare enviously at Florrie who is throwing loaded looks in Jake's direction, who in turn is making it obvious how much he has missed her.

Marcus is playing his part well, but I know it's all an act. He's been attentive, making sure I have a drink, enough to eat, and occasionally draping his arm around my shoulders while looking lovingly at me when his mother looks our way, and I wonder how long he can keep this up.

Just thinking of sharing a room with him is causing me anxiety because how will I maintain my indifference around him at such close proximity?

Finally, the welcome ordeal is over, and Camilla says reluctantly, "I'm sorry, guys, I have a yoga session with Ingrid to prepare for. Do you like yoga, girls? I'm sure she wouldn't mind if you joined us."

Jake scowls at his mother and pulls Florrie close to his side. "Back off, mum. I have plans for Florrie that don't include the lotus position, or the downward dog."

"Are you sure about that, Jake?"

Camilla laughs and I try to stem the giggle that my dirty mind is running with right now.

Jake just grins as Florrie blushes furiously and without a reply, they head outside.

Camilla giggles and I can't help but join her as Marcus rolls his eyes. "Honestly, it's like a playground in here. Come on, darling, we have a lot to do."

Once again, he reaches for my hand, and I hate the part of me that clings to it with every hope I've got because there is something so intoxicating about this man and it's probably because he's not interested in me in the way I want. It's a challenge I'm up for because I intend to creep into his mind and steal his heart from there. Discover what he likes, dislikes, and make sure I fit the puzzle. Sad really, but you can't help who you fall for and coming here has reminded me that Marcus Hudson is everything I put on my list for the perfect man, and I will not give him up without a fight.

CHAPTER 4

We step out into the bright sunshine, which reminds me how amazing this place is. The sun's rays touch the old stone building and wrap it in magic. The heady scent of the roses makes me want to linger and appreciate them, and spying a rusty bench under what appears to be an apple tree makes me long to grab my book and enjoy a peaceful hour or two, resting after the tiring journey.

It appears that Marcus has other ideas though and as we turn the corner, he drops my hand and says with pride.

"What do you think of her?"

Blinking in the sunlight, I see a bright red sports car gleaming as if it's fresh off the production line and he says quickly, "Jump in, I'll take you on a tour."

He opens the door like a true gentleman and as I slide onto the cool leather, I just hope my legs don't stick to the seat in this heat. I've never loved leather seats because it's like ripping off a band aid every time I try to leave.

Not this car though, it appears that even though the roofs

off, it has a state-of-the-art air conditioning system that wafts around my legs, cooling them to an even temperature.

Marcus slides in beside me and my mouth waters as his toned brown leg rests against the centre console and I physically ache to run my fingers through the soft dark hairs that look so tempting.

He removes some aviator shades from the glove box and my heart goes into free-fall, reminding me what a fool I am because a man like him would never really be interested in a girl like me.

As he starts the engine, he runs a cursory glance over me and just feeling it makes my heart melt into a puddle of lust. He frowns and I immediately think he's having second thoughts and is probably wondering why he has chained me to his side for the next two years.

Flicking open the box again, he removes a similar pair of shades and hands them to me with a gruff, "You can use these. The sun can be a little blinding. Do you have a tie for your hair?"

"Why?" I feel like a flustered fool as he reaches out and lets my long, blonde hair filter through his fingers and I hold my breath in case something like breathing could ruin this moment. "It will keep your hair away from your eyes and keep it tangle free."

Reminding myself how his man likes everything in his place, tells me the reason for his furrowed brow and it's doubtful it's out of concern for me, anyway.

I shake my head and say evenly, "No, I have one back at the house. I could run and fetch it if you think I should."

I feel as if I've failed because, knowing Marcus's dates, they probably have everything worked out already and wouldn't dream of leaving home without every eventuality catered for.

Once again, he reaches into the glove box and draws out

an elastic tie and smiles. "Here, you can use this. No need to go back to the house."

Reluctantly, I take the tie and wonder which of Marcus's girlfriends it belongs to. I'm guessing there have been many others sitting in this seat before me and I fight the wave of jealously it creates. Why am I acting like a lovesick fool since I met him? I'm not that girl. The one who draws hearts around our names with an arrow through them. Imagining my wedding as he gazes into my eyes and pledges his undying love for me. Planning our dream honeymoon and life together like his mother obviously has already. I'm not *that* girl and I need to remind myself of that and so I shrug and toss the tie back into the box. "I'm good thanks, elastic gives me split ends, anyway."

Pulling on the shades, I lean back and plaster on my disinterested face and take a deep breath because I will not fangirl after this man. If anything, I want it to be the other way around.

He eases the car into gear, and I cross my legs at the sight of those muscles flexing as he drives expertly out of the parking space, resting a broad muscular arm along the back of my seat as he turns to reverse. I bite my lip to stop my mouth from dropping open as he shifts the gears and as we tear off, leaving a trail of gravel behind us, my heart is galloping out of control.

When will I ever learn because almost immediately my hair is all over the place, obstructing my view? I try desperately to act as if I do this kind of thing every day as I fight mother nature and try to look chic and elegant in a wind tunnel?

Turning away from him, I peer through my hair to see a pleasant view of undulating hills and wildflower strewn verges. The sun is hot on my head and Marcus is right about the glare. Its rays heat my already burning skin as I gasp for air because this man drives like he's on a formula one circuit.

The bending roads are obviously no challenge to him as he expertly weaves his way around them, throwing me from side to side, as I cling on to the seat. I hate the fact my hair is dancing a crazy dance of I told you so and whipping my face with the slap I deserve for being so stubborn.

Marcus cranks up the music because conversation is limited and as the loud classical music fills the car, sounding like The Last Night Of The Proms, I feel as if I'm in a slightly weird film.

Picturing the effortless chic of Audrey Hepburn, faced with the reality of Thelma and Louise, I curse myself for not taking up his offer of the elastic tie, despite who wore it before me. Once again, she was probably sitting beside him, humming along to the track and resting her well-manicured nails on his knee as they tugged at his heartstrings.

I'm guessing she had one of those scarves that gently billow at their neck as the long end wraps around her head and had dark black shades to protect her eyes. Yes, whoever owned this elastic tie was winning at life and I'm just the reject who was available to step into the role as divorcee in waiting because as sure as I'm getting whipped by the wind on repeat, Marcus will sign those divorce papers exactly two years after we are married and breathe a sigh of relief that he made it through.

WE FINALLY STOP and it takes a moment to part the tangled hair that has woven a spider's web around my face, and I see a beautiful valley sparkling below us. We appear to be high on some kind of mountain, and I gasp in delight at the vista before me.

Marcus cuts the engine and for a moment, the only sound is my beating heart and the call of the birds circling overhead as everything becomes silent and calm and I take a few moments to catch my breath.

He says with obvious pride, "What do you think?"

"It's beautiful." The awe in my voice is definitely genuine because this place is paradise.

All around me, nature radiates her finest work and I stare in awe at the majestic landscape.

Marcus says with excitement, "Let's explore."

He exits the car and before I know it, is opening my door and offering me a helping hand as I step up to meet him. Hearing the rip of my rather sweaty legs off leather, I'm certain there are two massive red marks on my legs right now and vow to always walk behind him until they fade. Elastic woman probably wore a silk pant suit, or a long maxi dress and had no such trouble and just lowered her silk scarf and shook out her hair from that damned tie, before smiling as she took his hand.

"Over here, Sammy."

Shaking the hated image away, I note he's moved to the edge of a ridge, and I try to make my shaking legs work in order to join him.

Marcus looks a fresh as a daisy and from the sparkle in his eye and the smile on his face, he is in his element right now.

As I move to join him, I appreciate the long muscular tanned legs that emerge from his smart chino shorts and salivate at the rather tight t-shirt that clings to his muscles like I am aching to do. His deck shoes complete the look and I have never desired any man as much as I do him.

As I draw next to him, I see an amazing view below of an unspoiled landscape that stretches endlessly for miles, and

Marcus says gently, "Welcome to Dream Valley, Sammy. This is the land I was telling you about."

"Your land." I blink in surprise because it appears the Hudson family owns a small county because as far as I can see, there is nothing but green fields and undulating hills.

"Yes, below us is the Hudson inheritance. Acres of land all ripe for development."

My heart drops as I suddenly imagine a very different picture in a few years' time and say hesitantly, "What, this is your proposed development site?"

"Yes, impressive, isn't it?"

I'm at a loss for what to say because I'm horrified, actually. Just the thought of the bulldozers moving in and felling the trees that have stood proudly for generations makes my blood run cold. Seeing the rabbits playing in the field makes my soul break apart as the devil steps inside and takes a bite. Only now do I understand what I've done, what I have agreed to, because this is bad—very bad and the tears blind me as I struggle to form a reply.

Marcus laughs softly. "Yes, I see it all, a thriving community, houses, playgrounds, a village centre, connecting us to the local town, which already has a school, surgery, and church. Local people will be able to stay and not move from the area they have grown up in and the town will secure the future of Dream Valley for generations to come."

"But this will all go."

I can't disguise the horror in my voice as he turns and looks at me with an intense look and I almost shrivel up from the glare in his eyes as he says sharply, "Unfortunately, there are casualties of development. Remember, every town and every city were built on land like this. It's a necessary evil to ensure progression. To develop the land for the good of the people; our ancestors have been doing this for centuries and we are no different. We owe it to them to continue what we started, and this land is of no use to anyone other than my family and we need to allow it to be enjoyed by everyone."

His words sound noble enough, but a part of me dies inside as I stare at the beauty surrounding me. I know he's right to a point, but it still doesn't make me feel any better about my part in this. If I pull out, he will find another victim and I'm in no doubt about that. Then I think of his brother Dom and the reason he wanted to be first to claim this particular inheritance and I feel bad for a different reason entirely. Dom wanted to preserve this land for his family and generations of Hudson's to come and almost as if he can read my mind, Marcus growls, "Dom wants to keep this in the family. Greedily lock it away and deprive the town of developing into something better."

"Is that such a bad thing?"

My words slip out before I can check them, and he turns and takes a long hard stare that makes me shift on the spot. I'm not sure what's running through his mind right now but I'm guessing I wouldn't like it and yet, to my surprise, he lifts his hand and combs a tangle out of my hair with his fingers and just feeling the brush of his skin against mine causes any other thought to leave me immediately, except wanting more of the same.

He steps a little closer and smiles like Satan drawing another victim into his web of lies. "Maybe Dom is right. Maybe it's the right thing to do; carry on as before and continue living like the lord of the manor, allowing the locals to walk our land and admire a view they will never own. Turn away families who can't afford to stay here anymore and see the decline of our school and the surgery to close. The local shops will soon follow when those families move out and businesses fail, leaving only the local hotel and campsite to welcome in strangers who leave their litter and snap their photographs before leaving us behind—alone. Not everyone wants that, Sammy. I certainly don't. I love Dream Valley; it's my home and I want to ensure its future for generations to come. I know this is the right thing to do, no matter how much it hurts, because sometimes the best ways to heal is to cut out the cancer that's destroying us. The wounds will disappear, but there will always be a scar reminding you of what went before. I will bear that scar, Sammy, because I believe in Dream Valley. I will take full responsibility for breathing new life into a dying corpse and watch it rise like a phoenix from the ashes."

It's too much. I am blinded by him. He intoxicates me as his words push out every objection I have. Every word he speaks, every sentence makes me fall deeper, harder and crashing to the ground because how can I fight this—man.

He looks into my eyes and reels me in, and I can't think of anything but him at this moment in time. I know he's right. Yet I also believe Dom is right to want to preserve this land, but at what cost?

CHAPTER 5

Somehow, we make it back to the car, and I am riddled with uncertainty. Marcus broke the spell he had on me by pointing out his dream from his vantage point high on the ridge. A plan of houses and green spaces, ponds and nature reserves, intertwined with bricks and steel.

I could almost imagine the children playing in the parks and the women gossiping over their low, well-tended hedges with their neighbours. Their children walking to school with their friends and the parties that would bring the community together. Tucked away in the valley a short distance from Valley House, where Marcus's family would live. If I get my wish, that would also be my family, but could I live with what I sacrificed to get there?

The sports car makes short work of the track, and we soon find ourselves in civilisation as tarmac replaces rough ground and road signs replace rusty gates leading into fields.

"Where are we going?"

I finally speak and Marcus says in an even tone, "I thought you might like to see Dream Valley as it is now. It will give you more of an idea of my plans."

Once again, the classical music plays out like the Charge of the Light Brigade as we speed toward the place he says he wants to save.

The first thing I see is a sweet country church with a spire that catches the sun and calls to the congregation to gather. Marcus pulls up alongside it and cuts the engine. "St Thomas's has been here as long as Valley House. It was built by my ancestors and provided a place for the locals to meet and worship on Sundays. Local farmers mixed with gentry, and they were a small solid community. I'm guessing this land was once much like you've just seen but has earned its place here as the centre of the village for generations. Weddings, funerals and moments in time, marked out in some way by the prayers of the people. A place where everyone was equal and a place to worship, and I'm guessing that nobody was unhappy about that."

I know what he's doing, trying to show me how stupid my objections are. Refusing to acknowledge that, I shrug. "It's lovely, can we go inside?"

"Another time maybe, after all, we will be married here, so I'm guessing it won't be long before we are summoned to meet the vicar, Harrison Bowers."

My heart leaps and I mentally catch it as it falls. A church wedding. Why does that feel so wrong on every level?

"But I thought…" I'm at a loss for words and he laughs like an amused demon. "My mother wouldn't dream of a quick wedding at the town hall. She wants everything done the right way. You see, baby, the Hudson's have a particular role to play in Dream Valley and we must lead the way. The perfect model citizens who never step out of the image the locals expect of us, so hold on tight, you're in for quite a ride."

Almost as if he needs actions to back up his words, he

starts the engine and squeals away from the church, the sound of rubber on tarmac announcing our departure.

Before long, we stop outside what looks like a school and he points to the sign on the side.

Dream Valley Primary School. Headmaster Rufus Abel.

He laughs as he looks at the sign. "Rufus is a doddery old fool who lets the kids run rings around him. He's up for retirement but won't let go and you've got to either admire him for that or think him a fool."

"Why, he obviously loves what he does?" I feel myself rising to the stranger's defence, and Marcus laughs loudly. "What, delay a pension that he could never spend just to teach kids who don't listen to a word he says? No, he's not in their best interests and I should know because the old fool taught me back in the day."

"Wow, he's ancient then." I hit back with icy words and for some reason it sparks something in his eyes that makes my soul pant. Yes, Marcus likes to live on the edge of the abyss and I'm breathless at the fact he may well just tug me over with him.

"I'm guessing he will leave as soon as the new development goes ahead because he won't be able to cope with the new faces crowding his school. Another good reason to go ahead because my plans include extending the school and equipping it with all the latest gadgets needed to educate our kids the way they deserve."

Ok, my defences are crumbling around me as every word from his lips is like a wrecking ball to my objections. Part of me admires him for his dream. To make things better; drag Dream Valley into the modern world and make it thrive. But the rabbits, for goodness's sake, I can't bear the thought of them losing their homes. Then there're the hedgehogs, badgers and fairies that probably live by the sparkling hollows. What will become of them?

Closing my eyes, I need a moment to let insanity pass and when I open them, it's seeing his dark flashing eyes ripping my heart out and tying it in knots and his voice grows husky as he whispers, "Trust me, Sammy. I have it all worked out."

Once again, he starts the car and points out a small building as we speed past.

"Valley Surgery. I want to extend that as well and make it bigger, with better equipment and more staff. At the moment they can't cope with the few patients they've got, and we need to address that before it becomes more of a problem."

Now I know why Marcus has the planning committee in his pocket, because I feel like cheering him on like a desperate cheerleader lusting after the quarterback. As he points out the police station, fire station and ambulance, I start to see the bigger picture. We pass stone cottages along the main road that lead to other smaller roads where similar houses nestle in the valley. A small select community that has seen better days and I wonder what the people behind those doors will think of his plans. Not a lot, I'm guessing, because no one really likes change. It threatens and promises that things will never be the same again and destroys the utopia many believe they live inside.

Is progress really the best way? Should modern life really replace one that has served our ancestors well over time? Am I holding on to an ideal with rose-coloured spectacles because I'm in no doubt, if Marcus doesn't do this, somebody will? Maybe someone with less interest in the place. Someone who is lit up by greed and pound signs. Maybe this is in Dream Valley's best interests and I should stand beside my man and back him up. The sad thing is the only thing I can focus on is how good that sounds and not the problem of tearing apart the landscape.

My man.

How I love the sound of that.

CHAPTER 6

We finish off our tour by heading to the nearest town. I say town, it's almost a village because there are only a handful of shops resting on either side of a two-lane street. Cars can travel through and park outside the canopies of the small shops that open their doors and serve the inhabitants of the small and sleepy town.

The Cosy Kettle is the one that entices me the most, partly because of the brightly coloured flags blowing in the breeze and the wicker chairs set around small tables where the locals are enjoying coffee and cake in the pleasant sunshine.

We take one of the few spare tables and I'm conscious of the stares that follow Marcus wherever he goes. They appear as fascinated by him as I am, and I don't miss their not-so-subtle gazes in my own direction.

As we take our seats, a young girl rushes out to take our order and I see the hunger in her eyes as she smiles at Marcus and says coyly, "Mr Hudson, it's good to see you after your holiday."

"Thanks, Laura. I'll have an Americano and Sammy…" He looks across and smiles. "What about you, angel?"

Laura's eyes dart to me in surprise and I feel myself colouring up a little as I try to settle into my pretend role as Marcus's fiancée.

"A latte would be great, thank you." I smile warmly at Laura, who looks away, quickly scribbling our order down with an angry flush to her cheeks. Looking at Marcus, he is just staring out at the street as if she is of no importance, and I wonder if they ever had a fling. She looks to be around eighteen or nineteen and he is twenty-four, so maybe not. Then again, I'm guessing there's not much to choose from in this sleepy town and maybe age isn't a barrier when there isn't much choice.

She heads inside and Marcus looks content to sit among his people and bask in their admiration. Maybe it's the arrogance in him that keeps me keen because I love the fact he's so difficult to read.

Leaning forward, I claim his attention by saying with interest, "So, this apartment, where is it exactly?"

For a moment, he looks as if I'm talking in tongues and the frown on his face is quickly replaced by understanding and for some reason he looks away with a curt, "A little way from here. Like I said, it's not ready yet."

"But where exactly, can't we head there and see how things are coming along?"

Looking around me, it's doubtful it's around here because there's not a lot and certainly nothing that looks as if it's being converted.

"Maybe later."

He won't look me in the eye, and I feel the warning flags fanning the flames of my unease and like a dog with a bone, I hang on tight and say with determination, "When?"

"Your coffees, can I get you anything else."

Laura addresses her question to him, and he smiles at me with a look that could destroy any resistance I have toward him—if I had any, that is.

"Darling, can I order you something to eat? You must be hungry."

Looking inside, I see a display of cakes and fancies under glass domes and my mouth waters. "What do you recommend?" I smile at Laura, who shrugs. "I don't know what you like."

She chews on her bottom lip and looks so miserable I'm starting to think there is something I'm missing, and Marcus says loudly, "Allow me because I know what you like, darling." He winks and for some unknown reason, I blush because the look in his eyes should be marched straight to that church and forced down before the altar and cleansed with holy water.

I shift in my seat because I am affected by anything he throws in my direction and maybe the devil is in me too, because Laura is throwing imaginary daggers at my head right now, which brings out the worst in me.

Leaning on my hands with my elbows on the table, I bat my lashes at the man who plays games for fun and say huskily, "Chocolate. Lots of lovely smooth delicious chocolate that oozes sin and corrupts the soul. And cream. Whipped to perfection and nestling inside a biscuit that I could lick the length of and devour whole."

The lust in Marcus's eyes excites me so much I almost forget about Laura until she says dismissively, "We have doughnuts and flapjacks. Victoria sponge and brownies. The cream is off because we didn't get our usual delivery."

"What about a nice, delicious crumpet, dripping with butter, oozing from the holes in it?"

Marcus leans forward and whispers the request huskily as

Laura turns her attention fully on him and says, almost panting, "That could be arranged."

"Or a muffin, perhaps. Hard on the outside with a soft middle as you bite into it."

I lean forward even more and love the way Marcus shifts on his seat and a wicked grin tugs at the corner of his mouth as Laura snaps, "No muffins."

"Shame, I liked the sound of that." Marcus licks his lips and stares hungrily into my eyes and I stir my coffee with the long spoon and then lick the frothy milk off the end of it with a long, leisurely sweep of my tongue.

"Two crumpets it is then?"

Marcus stares at me long and hard as Laura moves away, scribbling on her pad with a snort of displeasure, as I replace my spoon and whisper, "Do you think that will get the tongues wagging?"

I cock my head in her direction and he reaches out and, to my surprise, grabs my hand and laces my fingers with his.

"Maybe we should just make sure. I mean, we do have a role to play, and we are in love after all—supposedly."

My heart quickens as he pulls me to meet him across the table and as his lips dip to mine, I taste the strong coffee on his. He licks the froth off mine and then, as my lips part, he ventures inside and wraps my tongue in his.

My heart is almost flatlining as I struggle to remain aloof about this but holy fish fingers this is the sexiest moment of my life, which reminds me how sad that life is when swapping saliva with a devil over a tearoom table is the highlight of it so far.

A surly cough makes us pull apart and Laura slams two plates between us and I blink in surprise because how long have we been connected? Surely, she hasn't toasted two crumpets and spread them with butter in the time we've been locked at the lips.

Marcus grins with a devilish glint in his eye as he stares at the Rolex on his wrist pointedly, and I feel the blush creeping through me as his meaning is clear. We were lost in a moment that turned into the longest kiss of my life.

Quickly, I grab the crumpet and, leaning back, take a bite, trying to stop my heart from thumping so violently as he does the same and smiles with appreciation.

"This is nice, don't you think?"

I briefly wonder if he means the Cosy Kettle, the crumpet or the kiss and just nod and say quickly, "Yes, I could get used to this."

He raises his eyes and I quickly look away because as sure as I'm drowning in lust for this man, I must remember that it's all an act and has the shortest shelf life before I'm tossed out with a smile of thanks and a new start in life—alone.

CHAPTER 7

We set off back to Valley House and Marcus takes a different route and as we speed along a coastal path; I fall deeply in love with Dream Valley. If anything, the surroundings reassure me I made the right decision in coming here, although the reason for it is slightly messed up, but I'm here now and sitting beside me is a man who intoxicates me in every way.

What am I going to do about Marcus Hudson because I'm at a loss right now? The fact my eyes devour him, and my senses are on high alert when he's near, tells me I have a huge problem. Two years stretch before me like a prison sentence because how can I possibly make this work? I know we will need to pull on all our acting skills and what about him? Can a man really play a part like this in public and then retreat in private? I'm guessing he's not short of female company, Laura, case in point and when he says with his husky drawl, "Are you ok, Sammy?"

I blurt out, "How will this work, Marcus?"

Just the slight tightening of his knuckles on the steering

wheel indicates his surprise, and he says slowly, "What are you thinking?"

"Well…" I take in a large dollop of air as my heart beats loudly. "I mean, what about girlfriends? Surely you have one, two, maybe a small harem?"

I laugh to disguise my anxiety and for a moment, that's the only sound as he appears to think long and hard about his answer.

As my question hangs awkwardly between us, I think I hold on to that dollop of air to keep me alive until he graces me with an answer, and then he sighs and pulls swiftly into a lay-by overlooking a sparkling sea.

Turning to face me, his eyes contain a storm I never saw coming, and he growls, "There are no girls, no one girl or even a gaggle of them. Only you."

"Me."

I stare at him in surprise, and he smiles, looking like every dream I ever had as he directs that soul shattering gaze to me.

"You're reacting to the rather cool welcome Laura gave you."

So, I was right, there was something between them.

"No, um, not really."

He leans closer and my words stop mid-air because I can't think of anything right now other than I want him to kiss me, really kiss me and mean it this time.

"Laura is annoyed at me for a different reason."

"What?"

"Before the cruise, I ran an advert in the local newspaper, advertising for the position I offered you. She applied."

"Oh."

He exhales sharply and looks irritated. "I interviewed her along with several others and wasn't that impressed with any of them."

"You say um, interviewed." Wondering if he means he interviewed them for the same position I sit in now, his fiancée. I feel slightly uncomfortable about that, and a smile tugs on the corner of his lips as he grins.

"Not exactly." He lifts my hand and studies the beautiful diamond that rests on the third finger of my left hand and, to my surprise, raises it to his lips and kisses it softly. "No, there has only ever been one contender for that position, but I'm guessing you may find a few Lauras dotted around Dream Valley who hope you fail."

I can't even worry about that because just the fact he KISSED MY HAND has me drooling at a moment, I couldn't have engineered if I tried.

"Why me, Marcus?" That's a question I've continually asked myself since he turned his attention to me the very first time we met on the cruise ship and he releases my hand and studies the beautiful view and looks a little confused, which surprises me, before saying softly, "I'm still working that out."

Sighing, he turns the keys in the ignition and as the engine roars to life, he says loudly, "I like you, Sammy. You make me laugh and you're easy to be around. Why wouldn't it be you?"

As we pull away, I'm left to digest his words as we pass spectacular scenery and I hate the fact a little niggling doubt is growing by the hour. Marcus wanted me because his brother did. It's obviously sibling rivalry at its most destructive. They both wanted the same thing—the Hudson land and I'm the gullible fool they thought would deliver it to them.

Thinking about Dom, I feel a little bad because at least he acted as if he genuinely cared for me and for a while, we were having a good time. He was one of seven dates I was paired with on the Cruising in Love programme, and I enjoyed his company. Then Marcus happened. Completely unexpected, like a heat-seeking missile aimed at my heart and even though he wasn't part of the programme, I followed him around like a lovesick puppy wagging its tail for only one master—him.

When he offered me the job as his property assistant, it was extremely good timing because I quit my job to go on the cruise. Then Florrie fell for his brother Jake, and everything slotted into place. Now I'm not so sure because it's one thing agreeing to a crazy scheme like this when high on holiday adrenalin, but it's another in the cold light of day.

Marcus stops the car in a lay-by on the edge of the road and says, "Come and see the most spectacular view in Dream Valley."

I scramble out of the car without waiting for him to open my door and follow him to the edge, where a small stone wall divides us from a gentle undulating hill filled with grazing sheep.

My breath catches as I stare down at a sandy beach that appears deserted and watch the waves rolling to shore and the noise of the surf reminding me what childhood holidays sound like and to my surprise, Marcus laces his fingers with mine and says softly, "I love this place. As children, we spent many hours on that beach. It's called Dreamy Sand beach and does exactly what its name describes. It's a place of dreams, adventures, and possibilities."

I keep quiet because I am learning a lot about Marcus in our trip around his memory and I can tell he holds a deep love for Dream Valley, which settles my heart a little.

How can his plans be wrong if he feels so passionate about this and for a moment every anxiety I have tumbles onto the beach below and is washed away in the surf?

"My brothers have their own agenda."

He sighs and grips my hand a little tighter. "Dom hates

change. He always has and would fight tooth and nail to hold on to the past and drag it into the future with him. I'm not saying he didn't like you, Sammy, but remember why we were on that cruise. All of us have a hidden agenda and I am just more open about mine. Dom wants the same thing—the land and the house and it's a race to the finish line. Don't underestimate either of us because we play to win. If you show him your mind is made up, don't show any sign of weakness, he will back off. However, if he thinks for one moment he still stands a chance of making you agree to marry him instead, he will seize it with both hands."

Now I feel even worse as he reminds me I'm just a pawn in a very sick game and I feel my heart hardening as I berate myself for the umpteenth time for being a grade A fool.

Suddenly, Marcus turns to stare into my eyes once again and tugs me closer to him. and says with so much sincerity, I'm reeled in again. "I just want to tell you I'm glad it's you. Happy you agreed and am looking forward to every minute we spend together."

He grips my hand tightly and whispers so softly, I strain to hear him. "In answer to your question, Sammy, there is no one else. I can't pretend there aren't a few ex-girlfriends lingering around Dream Valley, but that's what they are—ex. It may be uncomfortable for a while, but they will soon see that I've moved on and leave us alone."

"But…" I feel my face flush as I think about the more physical problem a man like that must have and wonder if he can put that aside for his dream and I hold my breath as a wicked glint in his eye tells me he knows exactly where my thoughts are heading and leans in and says huskily, "I'm a big boy now, Sammy. I can control my natural urges, can you, though?"

Pulling back a little, I blush furiously as he sees inside my soul as if he has a key to come and go as he pleases. "Of course I can."

Snatching my hand away, I let the wind whip around my face, slapping some much-needed sense into me and he laughs before adding, "I will enjoy watching you maintain control, Sammy, and look forward to you showing me how it's done."

"What do you mean?" I am genuinely confused, and he tugs me back against his chest and whispers, "Because it will be fun testing your resolve—and mine."

He steps back, leaving me feeling a wanton mess as my heart races with possibilities. Do I affect him—I doubt it, but he is a man after all and may be looking for a 'friends with benefits' kind of arrangement.

A girl can hope, anyway.

CHAPTER 8

Florrie looks at me with her eyes wide and her hand firmly clasped to her mouth. We are sitting on her bed, or I should say Jake's bed, as I fill her in on my day so far. Luckily, when we returned, Camilla was nowhere to be seen, and the guys had a personal fitness trainer booked and so I made the most of catching up with my friend by helping her unpack.

"What are you going do if he, well, you know, wants to take your relationship further? Please tell me you will guard your heart, Sammy, because I couldn't bear to find it broken one day."

Laughing, I shake my head. "Don't worry about my heart, Florrie. I'm just realising I have one. I mean, I've never been lucky in love, as you know, and this is just a continuation of that. What could go wrong? I mean, two years will pass by in a flash and then I'll have a new life here to keep me busy. Marcus told me he would make sure I had somewhere to live and a job and if that becomes uncomfortable, I could pack up and move on somewhere else. Maybe this will become my new business, 'bride for hire,' it has a catchy ring to it, don't you think?"

"No, I don't think."

Florrie looks at me in horror and makes me doubt my rash decision as she shakes her head sadly. "I don't want this for you, babe. I want the hearts, flowers, and dream. This is so cold and practical and, mark my words, nothing good will come from it. I mean, what if you find someone else you like in the meantime? What if he does? You would both be the talk of Dream Valley and not in a good way. Gossip can cut deep and I don't want that for you. Please re-think this, it's madness with disaster wrapped around it like poison ivy."

"Don't be so dramatic, Florrie, I'll be fine. I'm a modern woman with my future in my own fair hand. A man won't affect me at all, even an impressive one like Marcus Hudson. Anyway, what do you make of all this?"

I sweep my hand around the room and look at her with concern and she colours up slightly as she shrugs. "I don't mind."

"I bet you don't, you naughty girl."

"Well, Jake is rather gorgeous and he can't do enough for me. I'm looking forward to setting up here."

"What's your plan?"

Sitting on the edge of the bed, I gaze at her with curiosity and she smiles with a happiness I wish was mine right now. "Jake has promised to help me set up my business here. He's arranging for leaflets to be printed that we can drop around the village. Get the word out that a new beautician has arrived in town and has an opening special offer."

"Is there one here already? I can't see how two similar businesses would work."

She shrugs and folds a jumper for the third time already, as she appears a little lost in her own thoughts. I envy her that because it's obvious Florrie has fallen hard for the easy-going brother of Satan and I wonder if all the bad went into Marcus, reserving all the good genes for Jake because he is like a breath of fresh air in a room that chokes the life out of you when his older brothers are there.

Florrie shrugs. "Apparently, there's one other lady who operates a similar set up to mine. Grace Evans, I think she's called. Camilla told me about her when we finished up the sandwiches after Marcus dragged you off. Apparently, she's nearing retirement though, and Camilla told me that she was a member of her dominoes team and would 'have a word'. I feel bad about that. What if she's angry, and it makes things difficult for Camilla?"

Thinking of Marcus' adorable mother, I can't imagine anyone holding anything against her and I smile reassuringly. "You'll be fine. Maybe you could work together, help each other out. Offer to work with her rather than against her. It could work."

"Yes, I think it could. Anyway, what about you, didn't Marcus say something about an apartment and a job demonstrating his property empire? What's the situation there?"

"I'm not sure." I chew on a fingernail, a habit I have never really broken, and sigh. "It's weird, Florrie. I asked Marcus about the apartment and he said it wasn't finished. When we were in town, I asked if we could go and take a look and he was really dismissive. Do you think he's keeping something back?"

Florrie snorts loudly and I raise my eyes as she giggles. "That man holds secrets like the rest of us hold our breath. I'm guessing he is drowning in them and this is just another one. Jake told me not to trust a word from his lips because Marcus engineers everything to suit his purpose. Apparently, he's always been like that, calculating, planning and always getting what he wants. Not that Jake cares, of course, because he has different plans, but it's worth warning you of that so you can guard your heart."

She stares at me sharply, "And you will - protect your heart, because that man crushes souls for breakfast, apparently."

I feel even more uneasy after this conversation and wish my heart would stop bouncing around inside me like it's trying to make a run for it. Sighing, I lie back on the bed and look at the ceiling and wonder for the millionth time if this was such a good idea. Then again, what else did I have to come home to? No job and then no flat when I couldn't make the rent every month and no prospects. No, this was an unexpected lifeline that I grabbed with both hands because of him – Marcus Hudson. The man my body chose and my head went along for the ride. Maybe Florrie is right about one thing though. I must guard my fluttering heart because the cracks are already beginning to show and I can feel my resistance bleeding out through them.

∼

I LEAVE Florrie and head to Marcus's room and spend the next hour unpacking as I fill the space he created for me with my things. It feels so wrong on every level to be doing this at all and as I fill his masculine space with femininity, I wonder how this will work.

A gentle tap on the door shakes me out of my daydream and I'm pleased to see Camilla peering around the door as if she's afraid of what she will find.

"Darling, there you are. I've been aching for a word."

She heads inside and looks around with a slight shake of her head and wrinkles up her nose. "So basic, darling, I wish Marcus would allow me to unleash my designer urges and make this room prettier, more comfortable and less – soulless. I have a board for it already on Pinterest. I'm happy to share, if you can persuade him that is."

She appears thoughtful as she wanders over to the open window and says sadly, "Marcus is the one most like his father. Anthony was the same. Held everything in because he was the strong silent type. I never knew what he was thinking, even after bearing him four sons and devoting my life to him. You would think I had the measure of the man, but no, I never did. Marcus is like that. Closely guarded and always plotting some scheme or another. Wrapped in his own demons and I was hoping for a little sunshine to filter in through the crack."

She turns and smiles. "You are that sunshine, Sammy. I know it in my heart. The way he looks at you is different. I've never seen him look at anyone that way except for Molly of course."

MOLLY!!! Why is that name blasting around my head like a battle cry because surely this is the woman the elastic tie belongs to? I never pictured her as a Molly though, something way more elegant than that, but now I have a name to the image I feel my heart bouncing out of control yet again.

"Yes dear, so sad when she died. Terrible really. I never thought Marcus would get over it."

"Died! Oh no, what happened?"

I am actually horrified right now because my image has crashed and burned and I wonder if that was what happened. A road traffic accident maybe, perhaps Marcus was at the wheel and caused it. My heart is breaking for him as I imagine the court case, the funeral and the newspaper stories. Goodness, no wonder he's so closed off emotionally, it must be the trauma.

"I'm so glad I wasn't there when she died. It must haunt Marcus every day that he was powerless to stop what must have been a terrifying ordeal. We never did find her, you know. I sometimes think that Marcus hopes she'll just turn up one day. I know he was relentless in his search for her."

She was taken. Kidnapped by a travelling circus perhaps and is now some kind of trapeze artist with her memory wiped clean. A thousand possibilities race through my mind at a hundred miles an hour, but only one is causing my anxiety to blind me to anything else. What if she comes back to claim her man? At our wedding perhaps. Flinging open the door and striding down the aisle to claim her rightful place by his side. He will turn and start running towards her and I will be pleading with him not to leave me. I now have a migraine coming on as Camilla says sadly, "I think she's dead. Crawled off to Pineland Forest to die. She was fifteen after all and knowing her, she didn't want to put the family through the heartache. She was always considerate like that."

Now I'm confused and my mind has no scenario to explain this madness and Camilla sighs. "I offered to get him another dog just like her, but he growled there would ever be anyone like Molly and not to even try to replace her. I was worried for him, Sammy, for a long time. Marcus doesn't deal with grief well; it tears him up and darkens his aura."

Wow, he must have had a lot of grief in his life because Marcus wears a dark aura like most of us wear underwear.

Camilla smiles sweetly. "Anyway, enough about him. I'm guessing you only see sunshine and unicorns when he's around. Oh, to be in love, maybe I'll try it again. I have signed up for executive escorts. Maybe one of them will fall in love with me and we can have a double wedding."

She smoothes away an imaginary crease in the heavy curtains at the window, leaving me speechless. Executive escorts, wow, Camilla is a legend.

She smiles as she extends her hand. "Come and take a walk around the rose garden with me, darling. This room could use some nature to brighten it up. I'm thinking pink and white, such a delicious colour combination. Maybe you can persuade Marcus to redecorate with that in mind. It may help with his stress levels.

As her hand closes around mine, I feel a little shocked as I allow her to lead me out of a room that wraps me in shadows, like her son. Just picturing his face if I even suggested redecorating makes me laugh inside, and I wonder if I could have some fun with this after all. Crack the demon and make him bleed rainbows. It would be fun to try if nothing else.

CHAPTER 9

Camilla is such good company and I'm wondering if she's just grateful for some female company in a house that's bricks appear to be fashioned out of testosterone.

As I hold the trug while she snips the heady blooms from her rose garden, she chats about the house and how Anthony gave her free rein to develop the gardens and interiors.

"Such a happy marriage, darling."

She wipes a tear from her eye and smiles. "He was a commanding presence. He captivated everyone's attention when he walked into a room. Full of power and vigour. A man darling, not a wannabe like so many are these days."

As I follow her along the gravelled path with raised beds of roses on either side, I take a deep breath of luxury. With the sun beating down on my troubled head and the heady scent of nature filling my senses, I could be forgiven for thinking I had driven to paradise.

Camilla tosses a beautiful pale pink bloom to join the others and says wearily, "Let's take a moment, my knees aren't what they used to be."

Spying a bench set under another rose arbour, I set down the trug and sit beside her, grateful for the rest.

It feels so good to be here, despite the circumstances, and I picture my own little abandoned flat back home that has probably been rented out already. It seems a million miles away from Dream Valley and I hope that everything works out because just imagining leaving this heavenly place is already filling me with dread.

"So, tell me, darling, when is your family arriving?"

"Excuse me?" I feel my stomach roll as Camilla asks an innocent question that should have an easy answer.

"Oh, I'm, um, not sure really."

My mind is running to keep up because I never anticipated this question, at least for a few more hours and I'm not sure what to say as the lies swirl around inside me while I struggle to come up with a suitable answer.

The truth is, I haven't told them. My brother either. They would be absolutely horrified that I was planning on marrying a man I have just met and had packed everything up to come here. The fact I may have to admit failure two years down the line is a double blow I can do without and I just thought I'd carry on regardless and deal with it if it ever came up. I suppose I thought that 'what they don't know can't hurt them' and so I shrug and say absentmindedly, "I'm not sure, soon I think."

I feel like the worst human being alive as Camilla nods and says brightly, "I'll make up a room for them in the west wing. It's quite private and they can relax there without bumping into any of us.

Wondering why Florrie and I aren't sleeping there, I'm guessing it's to keep up appearances and I'm proved right as Camilla laughs softly, "The boys wouldn't hear of it when I suggested the same for you and Florence. Goodness me, in my day there was none of that, although between you and me…" She looks around again and whispers, "Anthony was an animal in bed and we made ours long before he placed a ring on my finger."

Her eyes burn brightly as she remembers happier times, and a wistful look passes across her face as she studies her wedding ring. "Don't get old dear, stay young at heart and live each day as if it's your last. I intend to do that; I always did, but I never knew Anthony's would be so soon."

"If you don't mind me asking, Mrs Hudson, what did he die of?"

She shakes her head sadly and says firmly, "Call me mother, or if that feels weird, Camother would be good, or Cammy, see what I did there."

She winks and I fight the giggle that threatens to ruin a serious moment as she sighs, "Cancer, darling, it got him good and proper. It's a terrible thing to watch a powerful man cut down by nature. Weakened and destroyed from the inside, both physically and mentally. You see, Anthony couldn't accept this was his time. He fought it like he did everything in life, but this was a fight he was never going to win. Watching him accept that and almost give into it made up my own mind to live for every day and make it count. I don't want to have regrets, Sammy, and I'm guessing you think that way too. I mean, you have fallen deeply in love with my son after just a couple of weeks and I admire you for that. Taking a chance on love even though it could fade after the excitement of meeting in the first place."

I'm sure I must have 'liar' written across my face as she grasps my hand and says gently, "If it's worth anything, I've never seen Marcus so happy. Unless you count the time he came first in the 100 metres sprint on sports day. Oh, there was also that time he bought his first little red sports car and took Belinda Harris out for a spin and from the looks on their faces when they returned, they had been on more than one ride."

She winks suggestively and says in a whisper, "I think that was the day he lost his virginity, a mother can always tell."

I actually feel sick thinking about Marcus and this harlot who gave it up for a quick spin around town.

Camilla sighs. "Mind you, I'm pretty sure they lost it years earlier. Those boys have a woman's scent mixed in with their libido. They're like dogs in heat, darling. Sniffing after every available bitch in the county and doing a good job of finding them. It's why Anthony made his will that way. Teach them the importance of family, settling down and staying faithful. Either that or risk all sorts of infections and a shotgun wedding to the first girl who fell pregnant. Oh well, that's all in the past now because he met you and fell in love and I also have Jake and Florrie to thank for the happiness I'm feeling right now. Two more to go and then I'm off the hook and can travel the world on the back of a camel."

"I'm sorry – what?"

She winks and looks around the garden, smiling with appreciation. "Yes, I will miss this place when I go travelling. I have it all planned out. Ride a camel, spend the night in the desert under the stars in a Bedouin tent, pan for gold and trek up a mountain. I crave adventure, Sammy. It's been festering inside me for far too long and soon I will be free to indulge my passions and I intend on starting with executive escorts. Do you have the time, by the way? I think my watch is a little slow."

Drawing my phone from my pocket, I can see it's nearing 6pm already, and she glances at the screen and says quickly, "Goodness, I need to get a move on. I'm double dating with Irene Jenkins tonight. We're heading out to dine at the Old Trout in Riverton."

"Riverton?"

"The nearest town with more than just a few shops. A virtual metropolis and I am heading there with a young man on my arm and a will to make this a night to remember."

"Um, that sounds…"

"Amazing, darling, utterly amazing, because I have been dreaming of this for years. Anthony always told me not to waste any time if anything happened to him and he should know. He made a habit of enjoying his freedom when he was alive, so don't think badly of me. This is my time and Irene is a regular. You should see the men she's 'dated' for want of a better word. She's showing me the ropes tonight, so I'm well practised in time for your wedding. I will be the talk of the town for more than one reason and I can't wait to see the drama that will bring."

I don't know what to say because it all feels a little inappropriate, really. I wonder what Marcus and his brothers will say when his mother walks down the aisle with a man the same age as them. Then again, I feel a lot of admiration for her too because why shouldn't she? Why not enjoy yourself when you have your freedom? I'm sure she deserves it, which tugs my mind back her comment about Anthony Hudson. Was he the cheating kind? I certainly hope not because, as Cammy said, Marcus is a lot like him.

CHAPTER 10

When I reach Marcus's room, I still can't think of it as mine, I head inside and almost faint on the spot. The man himself is standing in nothing but a towel, dripping from the shower and looking like every dream I've ever had.

"Oh, I'm sorry, I'll…"

"It's ok, Sammy, come in. I'll finish up in the bathroom."

He heads inside, leaving me in a state of shock because how will this work? It's so intimate and so wrong on every level. It's only now the facts are dawning on me what this room sharing will involve. I'm used to sharing. I have with Florrie lots of times but never with a man. I'm not sure how to deal with this and feel madly out of my comfort zone.

As soon as he enters from his bathroom, I say nervously, "So, the apartment. How long exactly?"

Hating the fact my voice sounds incredibly high, I don't miss the flash in his eyes as he senses I'm not really that comfortable with this and who can blame me. Marcus is a powerful man for a variety of reasons and the main one being the fact he is all man, from his rippling biceps, the smattering of dark hair on a chest that demands attention and the hard look in his eyes as he maintains an aura of control.

However, he now apparently can't look me in the eye as he turns away and reaches for his watch, before strapping it on his wrist with a slight shrug of his shoulders. "I told you, it's not ready. I'm not sure how long it will take, but it suits our plans, anyway."

"Our plans?" Unaware we had made any concerning our sleeping arrangements, I look at him in confusion and he sighs. "The fact is, we are engaged and soon to be married. How would it look if you were living elsewhere? Mum would be suspicious and the locals talk. Obviously, the sooner we can arrange the wedding, the better because then we get the land and can start the ball rolling to get planning permission. It's just easier this way and like I said before, if you're uncomfortable with that, I'll sleep on the floor or the sofa."

He looks at me with a curious look in his eyes and for some reason the enormity of what I've agreed to takes me by surprise. Suddenly, everything flashes before me in fast forward as I see the ship where we met and the excitement of that. The engagement at sea and the tour he took me on today. I picture his mother in her 'mother of the groom' outfit walking down the aisle with her 'date' and then I see the disapproving look of my bridesmaid Florrie and the empty space where my mother would be sitting in the church. Imagining walking down the aisle, probably with one of Marcus's brothers on my arm instead of my father, tears at my heart and then there's him. The man I foolishly let talk me into this, watching me like a hunter with a deer in its sight.

He is all encompassing. I can't breathe when he's around and I would like to say I agreed to all of this out of a sense of adventure and with a cool head. But I didn't. I couldn't wait to wear his ring on my finger because I am that desperate for love – for him. I don't even know him – not really, and I have agreed to something I'm not sure I can live with.

As my mind spirals out of control, the only thought I'm clinging on to is the fact I thought I'd have my own space – away from him but obviously not. My life is a ticking bomb and I can see it exploding at the most awkward moment and my legs shake at the scale of the mess I've got myself into.

However, as I inwardly melt down, he reaches out and catches me before I even hit the ground. Strong arms grip mine and pull me close and I'm surrounded by the scent of a powerful relaxant as he holds me close and whispers, "It's ok, I've got you."

Trembling slightly, I cling to him and love the way he holds me close while I press my heated face to his chest and hear the steady beat of his heart as he brings me back from complete and utter madness. Squeezing my eyes tightly shut, I try to breathe and compose myself because as panic attacks go, this one has surprised me. It came out of nowhere and proves to me I shouldn't be doing this because if this was right, I should be floating on air.

Marcus pulls me down beside him on the bed and says with a slight edge to his voice, "I'm sorry, Sammy,"

"For what?"

"For dragging you into this madness. I know I'm asking a lot of you, too much probably, but I'm being driven by desperation."

Now I feel even worse as he reminds me I'm only here because he's desperate and he wouldn't look at me twice if he didn't have a hidden agenda.

His husky voice filters through my crowded thoughts, and he says sadly, "I never wanted this. To be honest, I always thought I'd never marry. I couldn't see myself making that commitment and always kept away from emotions and feelings, preferring to throw myself into building my property empire instead."

He shakes his head. "Then my father died and left behind a cruel last punch. The only way I could guarantee my dream was to indulge his."

He sighs and you could hear a feather hit the carpet as the silence waits in anticipation for his next words and he laughs again with a bitterness that makes me sad for a whole different reason.

"You've met my mum. She deserves the best of everything because she devoted her entire life to my father and her kids and always tried to look happy. But I heard the arguments, the tears and the slamming doors. In fact, I used to listen out for them when we were sent to bed every night. Despite what she tells you, it wasn't a happy marriage because of him."

"Your father?"

He nods. "He was controlling, coercive and a manipulator. Not great qualities and I'm doing my best not to copy them. Mum put up with him because of us. Because she would never leave and he treated her like the hired help. Even when he got sick, she fussed over him and would never say a bad word about him. You see, my mother has all the qualities I admire in a person and yet despise at the same time."

He looks directly into my eyes and my heart bleeds for him because I see such sadness there, I can almost touch it and he sighs heavily. "I didn't want to be him, Sammy, but I could be. You see, I'm like him in lots of ways. Hard on the outside, with not a lot inside but a desire for power, for success and a ruthless streak that gives me what I want. I know I was wrong to drag you into this madness, but for some reason it had to be you."

"Why?" I whisper the word and he grasps my hand and

squeezes it tightly and I feel the desperation inside him. "I don't know. Something clicked when I met you and when Dom told us of his plans to persuade you to choose him on that infernal programme you all signed up for, I knew I couldn't let that happen. You were mine, not his. Does that make me sound mad because I think I might be?"

I'm not sure how to answer that question, and he grips my hand a little tighter. "I'll completely understand if you're having second thoughts. I would myself, but in helping me you are doing an amazing thing. Think about the people, Sammy. The families and the lives they could live here in Dream Valley. The laughter, the celebrations and the sense of community that is slowly diminishing over time. Then think of that gorgeous space I showed you today. Empty except for nature. Beautiful, magnificent, and unspoilt for generations to come. Dom is right to want to preserve it, but at what cost? Soon the village will die, shops close, the school will lose it children and the people will move on because the area has nothing to offer them but a great view. We need more than that and I recognise it. Dream Valley will still be a beautiful place to live. I will make sure of that but it will still have a beating heart."

The picture he paints is a good one and I understand why he wants to do this, but can I do this? Walk down the aisle with a virtual stranger in the name of adventure?

"Think about it, angel. Take your time, but know I'm doing this for all the right reasons. Help me and I'll make sure you're ok. I always will."

A loud knock on the door makes us both jump and Camilla heads into the room, making our jaws drop.

She is dressed to impress alright and I stare in admiration as she stands before us in a black knee length dress and stilettos, her hair brushed and slightly wavy at the ends with her make-up looking as if she's had it professionally done and a scarf slung around her neck offering a bright splash of colour. She is clutching a bag and holding her phone, and she smiles happily and winks as she sees Marcus's hand still in mine.

"Sorry to barge in, darlings. I really would get a lock on that door – just saying." She winks at Marcus and I feel my face burning as she says airily, "I'm off to the Old Trout for dinner. So sorry to leave you alone on your first evening, Sammy, but Irene is off to see her daughter in Edinburgh tomorrow and this was my last chance to be shown the ropes."

Marcus winces as she laughs softly. "I still can't believe I'm doing this. It feels strange after so long. Do I look ok?" She twirls on the spot and I'm surprised to hear the warmth in Marcus's voice as he says sweetly, "You look beautiful, mum, you'll knock them dead."

"Ooh, let's hope not, darling. I've had enough death to last me a lifetime."

She giggles and then sighs wistfully. "Are you sure you're ok with this? It must feel strange watching your mother head off on a date."

"Of course I am, you deserve it."

"Thanks, darling."

I watch in fascination as Camilla's eyes water and she sniffs, a soft laugh disguising her obvious emotion.

"Oh well, here goes nothing. Don't wait up."

She winks as she spins on her killer heels and makes it out of the room and I stare at Marcus in shock. "Are you really ok with her, um, dating?"

"Why not." He shrugs and holds my hand even tighter, reminding me he hasn't let it go for a second. "I told you, she has put her life on hold for far too long and she has my blessing to live it hard while she can."

"You surprise me, Marcus Hudson." I stare at him with a smile and he looks confused. "Why?"

"I don't know, maybe there's more to you than people think."

He shakes his head and I watch the cocky player in him return with a vengeance as he growls, "I'll deny everything if you tell a living soul. Now, come on, I've booked us a table at the local restaurant. The Olive Tree. I hope you like Italian."

He jumps up and pulls me with him and once again, looks at his watch. "You have exactly thirty minutes to change and meet us downstairs. I'll give you some privacy."

"We?"

"Jake and Florence."

Feeling relieved about that, I wonder when I'll run into his brother, Dom, because I'm not looking forward to that conversation one bit.

CHAPTER 11

I decide on a simple white shift dress and wedge heels and grabbing my bag, head off to meet the others downstairs.

As I walk along the impressive hallway, I admire the intricate wallpaper and the scent of roses in the air. Camilla obviously likes to run an orderly home and it feels good to be here. Then again, it would also be good to have our own space because I haven't relaxed for a minute since we arrived.

The staircase leading down to the hallway is edged with family photographs in matching black and white frames and I smile as I see a lifetime of memories lining the route. Marcus as a small boy in a line with his brothers. Family holidays and baby pictures, alongside school days and holidays.

Stopping for a moment, I stare at one of them as a family and see a man a lot like Marcus looks now, standing with his arm draped across the shoulders of a youthful Camilla Hudson. Peering closer, I stare into a pair of eyes identical to his and my breath hitches as I see the family resemblance. Even from here I feel the power of Anthony Hudson. From the way his wife gazes up at him in adoration, to the smiles on the faces of his offspring. But on closer inspection, I see a picture that appears engineered for appearances sake and I wonder if I'm letting Marcus's story influence me. Maybe it's because it seems too perfect, too contrived. It's as if everyone is on their best behaviour just for the photograph. The fact they are standing so still, in identical poses with straight backs and none of the chaos that I'm sure having four young boys brings tells me that.

"Take a good look, Sammy."

The heated whisper at my ear makes me jump and startled, I knock into a hard body behind me.

Two strong arms reach out to steady me and my heart sinks when I see exactly who it is.

"Dom." I whisper his name as if he's the 'one who can't be named' and I'm about to be struck down by the dark lord himself.

His stormy expression makes my heart lurch inside me as he says angrily, "Take a good look at the photograph, and see what you've signed up for. My brother is the exact replica of our father and you have just sold your soul to the devil and if you want to know what that feels like, just ask my mother."

My breath hitches at the venom in his words and he growls, "If I were you, I'd run as fast as you can away from the big bad wolf who will eat you up and spit out what's left."

"Um, well, thanks for the advice but I really should…"

He slams his hands either of side of me against the wall, trapping me in a wall of muscle and hisses, "Why did you choose him over me?"

"Because…" My voice tails off because I don't know what to say. Why did I?

I mean, Dominic Hudson is an attractive desirable man, a lot like Marcus. He has the same dark edge, unlike their other two brothers Jake and Brad who appear to have inherited more of their mother's genes. If any of them, I should have tried with Brad, although he didn't seem that interested.

Licking my lips nervously, I shrug. "Because it just happened, I suppose. We were having a good time and I loved getting to know you but when Marcus told me about your plan to seduce me and make me marry you instead, I felt a little disappointed."

"Disappointed."

He barks out a laugh and I stare at him angrily. "Yes, I thought you liked me – for me. Not because you wanted to trick me into a crazy plan to claim your inheritance."

"So, you thought you'd do it anyway, with my brother. So much for your principles."

Standing tall, I look him in the eye and try to regain the moral high ground by saying with a sharp hiss, "For your information, I chose Marcus because he was honest with me. At least he never pretended to actually like me and try to make me fall in love with him. He was upfront from the start and I like that."

Dom shakes his head and doesn't appear to be in any hurry to release me from my muscle-bound prison and I almost jump as he hisses, "So you would go along with his plan to destroy our home, wipe away years of history, years of protecting the environment and years of tradition for what – money, prospects, a future?" He rolls his eyes and leans closer. "I did like you, Sammy, I still do and I hate to see you falling for his lies."

"What lies?" I hold my breath as his eyes glitter and he says tightly, "My brother will say just about anything to get what he wants and he always has. He won't think twice about using you for his own agenda and that's what angers me the most. I really like you, Sammy. We had fun, we still could. Help me preserve this amazing place and keep our family home intact. Don't let years of history crumble for financial gain and stay with me and see if we can make this marriage work. Marry me, Sammy and I will spend my life trying to make you happy. Raise a family here, in Valley House surrounded by family and a life many can only dream about. Change your mind and head Marcus off at the pass because he will ruin you, plain and simple and I can't stand by and watch that happen. He will tear down your walls and rebuild them on land that should be protected. He is a greedy, arrogant man, who tells you what you want to hear while doing what the hell he wants."

"Sammy!"

I jump as Marcus's angry voice reaches out like a knockout punch and Dom laughs softly before turning away from me and staring down the staircase at his brother who is looking mighty pissed off.

"What's the matter, bro, are you worried that she'll ditch you for me. I know what that feels like by the way."

Edging past him, I almost run down the stairs and catch hold of the hand Marcus offers me. Pulling me to his side, he says nothing but leads me outside to a waiting Range Rover, with Jake at the wheel and Florrie sitting beside him in the front passenger seat.

Maybe she can see my heightened colour as I try to deal with what happened because she looks concerned and I smile weakly as Marcus helps me into the car before sliding in next to me.

"Sorry I'm late." My voice is breathless, as if I've run a marathon and as I struggle with the seatbelt, I can't shake the angry scene from my mind.

Strong hands reach out and fasten me in and a soft voice whispers, "It's fine, Sammy."

To my surprise he kisses me softly on the cheek before fastening his own seatbelt and saying tersely, "We should go, the table's booked for seven."

Luckily, Jake's voice interrupts the madness as he starts to point out various places to Florrie giving me precious time to lean back, close my eyes and catch my breath.

I knew it was only a matter of time before Dom cornered me but just thinking of the picture and his vicious words, tells me I've stepped into a family feud that can only end in tears.

CHAPTER 12

The Olive Tree is a sweet Italian restaurant on the edge of the small town we visited earlier. Twinkling fairy lights are wrapped around every post and candles burn in steel lanterns on a porch that creaks under our weight as we venture inside.

Soft classical music plays from hidden speakers and I immediately know why Marcus chose this place because it's him all over. The soft, seductive ambiance with the lilting classical music to serenade the senses.

Walking in with him is like holding the hand of a mafia don because every eye in the place turns and watches us approach. Maybe the Hudson brothers are what passes as royalty or celebrities around here because I don't miss the fascination in the eyes watching our small group with interest.

Suddenly, I hear a soft seductive voice whisper huskily, "Marcus, it's been a while."

Looking up, I see an attractive woman with dark wavy hair and amazing green eyes. Her clothes are moulded to her body like Jessica Rabbits and the way she is looking at Marcus she has an interest in him that bothers me – a lot.

"Maria." He nods and I don't miss the smirk on Jake's face as he looks between them and the warning bells start ringing loudly in my mind.

Maria completely ignores everyone else and edges closer to him, despite the fact he is firmly holding my hand and she says seductively, "You never called."

I can sense Florrie's disapproval from here and feel so miserable as I am practically invisible right now and don't really know what to do.

Marcus pulls me forward and says gruffly, "Have you met Sammy, my fiancée?"

Maria's eyes slide over to me and I almost jump back at the venom in them as she drawls, "Is that right?"

It feels a little awkward as she looks me up and down and the slight sneer on her lips is like a well delivered blow to my ego, so I straighten up and smile with a promise in my eyes telling her to back off before she gets hurts and say icily, "I'm pleased to meet you, Maria. You have a lovely restaurant."

"Yes, I do."

She looks back at Marcus and I see the storm in her eyes as she says tightly, "I'll arrange for Genevieve to show the rest of your party to your table, if I may have a word – in private."

She almost hisses her request and I half expect a mafia hitman to take me out in one swift move as she mentally takes a contract out on me and Marcus says in a bored voice, "I'm sorry, Maria, business will have to wait. I'm off duty and just want to enjoy time with my girlfriend and family. Make an appointment with Sammy tomorrow, usual office number."

I stare at him in surprise because this is the first I've heard of the office and for some reason I'm happy about that.

Finally, a real purpose for being here and from the look in Maria's eyes, she is not happy at being asked to go through me. I just hope she's not making my food because it may be tampered with in revenge.

Marcus lifts my hand and kisses it and as the ring sparkles in her face, I see the fury reflected in her eyes which makes my heart sink. Does every woman in Dream Valley hate me already? It certainly feels that way and I wonder if Maria was another applicant for the position I now hold.

As we take our seats at a pleasant table by the window, Florrie whispers, "Wow, that was intense. Do you think they…?"

She nudges me and I say in a tight voice, "Probably, and I doubt she's the last one I'll meet."

Florrie looks worried but is soon distracted by Jake as he talks her through the menu with one arm casually slung along the back of her chair.

Reaching for my own menu, the words blur in front of my eyes as I feel like the most unwelcome stranger in town. Is this my life flashing before me? Everyone desiring what's mine and waiting for an opportunity to take it for themselves. Dismissing me out of hand as Marcus indulges in his own desires, apparently like father like son.

Thinking of Camilla living like this makes me feel sad for her and I wonder if she experienced nights like these. What about when he was away from home; did she wonder who he was with while she bathed her sons and read them a bedtime story?

Glancing across at Marcus, he is studying the menu with a bored air of arrogance and I see several people gawping at us from the other tables. Sighing, I try to distract my mind from how crazy my life is right now.

Genevieve returns to take our order and after much deliberation, we finally settle on shared appetisers and pasta dishes for the main course. Marcus orders champagne and a non-alcoholic beer for Jake and we make small talk while we wait.

Occasionally, I glimpse Maria watching us with a fierce expression as she moves around the restaurant but Marcus ignores her which must be a blow to her ego.

"A toast."

I look up in surprise as Marcus holds up his glass and smiles. "To Sammy and Florence and our new lives together."

Jake grins and clinks his beer with Florrie's glass of champagne and adds, "To having fun and living our best lives."

He swoops down and kisses her softly and I feel a little envious of my friend because this is real, for them, anyway. Marcus whispers in my ear, "Sorry about, Maria, she was a little cool towards you and you must be wondering why."

"Oh, it's fine, no worries." I try to brush it off and he says with a little irritation, "She asked for my advice a few weeks ago because she wants to extend the restaurant and knows I have contacts in the planning department. The trouble is, she insists on doing it at her house one evening over dinner. I couldn't think of anything worse to be honest and have been putting her off. I had to be abrupt with her to drive the message home but it appears you bore the brunt of that and I'm sorry."

Looking past him, I see Maria throwing imaginary daggers at me and sigh inside.

Luckily, the food looks edible when it arrives and is really lovely. I must have been hungry because I manage to polish it off and feel quite tired by the time I finish. Maybe it's the wine, the fact I couldn't eat another thing, or that I was up at the crack of dawn and travelled for several hours to get here without catching my breath until now.

Suddenly, Marcus's phone rings and he looks at the screen with a frown and answers with an urgent, "Is everything ok?" Jake looks across with interest as Marcus rolls his eyes and says wearily, "It's ok, mum, where are you?" Florrie looks at me with concern and I see Jake's easy-going expression change like the wind, into one of worry and concern.

Marcus just nods and shakes his head as he says gently, "Stay where you are. Jake will come and get you, just give him thirty minutes. Maybe wait in the restaurant and grab a coffee."

He cuts the call and Jake groans. "The car?"

Marcus nods with a grin, "Of course."

"Oh, for goodness's sake, that bloody car."

Jake grabs his keys and Marcus says gruffly, "I'll settle up. Sorry it's your turn, we'll call a cab."

Jake rolls his eyes and turns to Florrie.

"Sorry babe, we need to go and tow mum home – again."

"What do you mean – again? Is she always breaking down then?"

Jake grins and starts to laugh as Marcus says with a sigh, "Our mother has discovered her inner environmentalist and has 'gone green', as they say. Shortly after our dad died, she celebrated, for want of a better word, by buying an electric car. Not even a hybrid. Full on electric, which would be fine if she remembered to charge it. For some reason she forgets it actually needs plugging in and this is her standard rescue call when she runs out of power and needs a tow home."

Struggling not to laugh, Florrie catches my eye and grins as they head off on their rescue mission and Marcus raises his hand and beckons Genevieve over and asks for the bill.

As she heads off, he takes out his phone and I hear him arrange a cab and as we wait, he says with a sigh, "You'll get used to my mother, angel. She's a little scatty but is easily forgiven. No matter how hard I've tried, she just can't plan ahead and just heads off on some crazy scheme without even thinking of what could happen."

"Maybe you should check her car every night then and give her a helping hand."

"You're right. I should just do it myself, but last night it was Brad's turn to check, and he's just as bad as she is."

Genevieve heads over with the card machine and as Marcus settles up, I reach for my purse because I hate just assuming that he will pay for me and as I hold out my card, he waves it away.

"Not required, angel, for anything?"

"No, I need to pay my way, please let me chip in."

His strong hand closes over mine and pushes it down on the table and he smiles into my eyes, making me feel very warm inside.

"No need, I'll pay. After all, I will be paying your wages from now on, anyway. Call it a perk of the job, a sort of lunch allowance. Maybe that will make you feel better."

"Not really, but thank you. However, just so you know, I will be paying my way from now on, regardless of who pays my wages."

He nods and winks and as we head to the door, I say impulsively, "The cab then, I'll pay for that."

"Ok, fine." He shrugs as if it's of no consequence and I feel pleased that I've won this one at least.

I follow him out with an imaginary knife sticking into my back that Maria has carefully placed there as she watches us go with a frown and something tells me I should get used to this.

CHAPTER 13

The taxi arrives about twenty minutes later, and I doubt there's much demand for them in Dream Valley. It's hardly the metropolis and as we head outside, I'm surprised to see a landrover that has definitely seen better days waiting for us.

Trying to disguise my surprise, I smile at the rather rough looking man leaning against it, dressed in an open-necked checked shirt and dirty jeans, watching us approach. He nods as Marcus says respectfully, "Evening, Jim, thanks for this."

"No worries, son. Always happy to help."

Marcus catches my eye and grins before opening the door and helping me into a car that has definitely failed its MOT, just by the fact there are no seatbelts!

Marcus jumps in beside me and is obviously finding this funny as Jim opens the driver's door and prepares to start the engine.

I stare at Marcus pointedly and he shrugs before grabbing hold of my hand and whispering, "You can hold on to me if you like, although it's doubtful you'll need to."

He is trying not to laugh at the expression on my face as I

hope to God I'm not sitting in something that smells like I might be. In fact, I need to hold my breath because this car smells atrocious, as if it has never been cleaned and I'm sure I can see hay tucked inside one of the cracks in the back of the seat in front of me.

Jim starts the engine and checks over his shoulder, before pulling away.

I'm glad it's not far and wonder if this is just a favour he owes Marcus, because this can't be a cab company, surely.

As the car moves off, I'm amazed to find we don't appear to be moving that fast. In fact, I don't think he even shifts gear as we crawl at a snail's pace along the road.

Marcus checks his phone and says loudly, above the roar of the clunky engine, "It looks as if Jake's nearly there; they've made good time."

"Your mum broken down again?" Jim yells in his slow drawl and Marcus nods.

"Usual story, Jim."

"She should have bought a landrover. They never fail, are always reliable and a damn fine ride."

That's definitely a matter of opinion, and Marcus laughs as I raise my eyes and shake my head.

"Is this your lady, Marcus?"

"Yes, this is Sammy."

"Hi, darlin', welcome to Dream Valley."

"Thanks, um, Jim."

I'm feeling a little worried about Jim's car because I could walk faster than he's driving, and he hasn't even made it out of first gear yet.

"Trudy was telling me you were getting married, couldn't believe it myself."

Marcus nods. "I'm full of surprises."

"If you need transport to the church, I'd be honoured."

Quickly, I look at Marcus in horror and he grins, a hint of the devil flashing in his eyes. "I'll think about it, thanks."

I'm not sure what's happening here, but this car is not fulfilling its role in life as we bump over every stone on the road, almost in slow motion. I'm wondering if this is just a joke and they will burst out laughing at any minute and speed off into the darkness.

I'm not sure what to say because I don't want to be rude, but my mind is screaming at this man to put his freaking foot down. I have had a very emotional day, and this is not helping my stress levels and yet Marcus just leans back and closes his eyes, making me wonder if we're here for the night. I could take a long-haul flight to Sydney in the time this is taking, and it's so frustrating.

Jim starts singing 'Rockstar' by Nickelback and he wouldn't be winning any karaoke or X Factor contests with his rendition. It is actually hurting my ears and we are still in the same street he collected us from.

Nudging Marcus, he opens his eyes and smirks as I mouth, "What the…?"

He shrugs and closes them again, leaving me wondering if I should just open the door and sprint up the hill to Valley House. I'd certainly get there a great deal sooner.

Suddenly, Jim makes a sharp turn and my face meets the slightly sticky glass as I'm thrown against it and he says irritably, "Bloody foxes."

Then, to my horror, he reaches down on the floor beside him and pulls out a shotgun and, opening the window, proceeds to fire off several rounds into the bushes. I jump in fright and almost climb onto Marcus's lap as my whole body shivers with nerves and disbelief. It's now official. I'm in a car with a psychopath and I'm not sure which of these two men I trust the most.

Marcus wraps his strong arms around me and holds my head to his chest, whispering, "Don't worry, it's just Jim."

Just Jim, is he kidding? Just Jim could be the next Freddy Kruger, Hannibal Lecter, or that guy from The Shining. Just Jim is seriously off his head and we are paying for the pleasure!

Jim mumbles curses and tosses the gun to the floor and I almost expect it to fire off a few angry rounds for good measure and as we start again, I pray for deliverance and not the film version either, because surely, I have walked into hell right now.

"You busy, Jim?"

Marcus asks a question and I wish he would just shut up because I don't want to remind Psycho Jim, we are here at all and Jim says loftily, "Always busy, Marcus, crops to grow and harvest and cows to milk."

Marcus whispers, "Jim's the local farmer and owns Dream Valley farm. His cab business is something he set up for the evenings. He's used to driving an ancient tractor and doesn't differentiate when he's in a car."

"Hey Sammy." I jump as Jim remembers I'm here and the fact he remembers my name is seriously worrying. "Get Marcus to bring you to the farm. Trudy would love to meet you and show you around. We slaughter our own meat, you know; you could help if you like."

Marcus's shoulders shake as I stare at him in horror and hold on just a little tighter. "Oh, um, yes, lovely, thanks."

Marcus squeezes me and says loudly, "We'll let you know when, though, Jim. Sammy is working for me and starts tomorrow. Plus, there's the wedding, so it may have to wait awhile."

I actually think I love Marcus Hudson. He has ridden, or at least walked in slow motion, to my rescue and I owe him for this – big time and Jim shouts above the rattle of the engine. "Understood. So how are things with your plans, all good?"

"Yeah, we're meeting the vicar tomorrow after work. I think mum's got the rest planned."

"Trudy could help if you like. She makes a mean fish stew."

"Thanks, I'll let you know."

Marcus physically shakes with laughter as I pinch him hard and tightens his hold, reminding me I'm still sitting on his lap like a child.

Far from worrying about that, I'm enjoying the experience because I am that deluded, and that sad. Any form of contact with the usually cool character I have agreed to help out is welcome and yet tonight I have seen a side to him I like. He's relaxed, probably due to the wine, and I like it. Despite the fact I'm on the road to hell with a fox/cow murderer, I'm enjoying the experience.

We finally make it out of the high street and start the excruciating climb up the hill to Valley House. Wondering if we might make the sunrise by the time we reach the top, I content myself with snuggling into Marcus's arms and enjoying the experience. I even close my eyes and take deep breaths of a scent that is fast becoming my favourite one and as Marcus leans back and the car bumps on just about every stone in sight, I feel happier than I have for some time.

Sleep is impossible, so I just close my eyes and try to block out the nightmare journey and for a moment I feel quite at peace with the situation. Despite the fact that Jim is certifiably insane, at least he is friendly, which is more than can be said for the women of the town.

The fact that Marcus is stroking my arm is nice, soothing even and just feeling the heat of his body through his thin shirt, is wrapping me in comfort and a place to call home. Marcus is now my new best friend, my pretend lover, and my employer. We must work as a team and work fast because two years could be easy or hard, depending on how we set the rules in place. Pondering what that future will hold is still unknown, but somehow that makes it even more exciting.

As the car climbs, I wonder if it will make it to the top at all because it almost feels as if we're standing still. The engine is screaming and Jim's singing is louder and I have a definite headache coming on. Marcus is apparently sleeping, although that's doubtful, because I'm guessing he can only sleep in his coffin because he's obviously some kind of demented demon for putting me through this agony.

We finally make it to Valley House, approximately one hour after we started out and remembering my promise, I say tentatively, "Um, how much do I owe you?"

Marcus says quickly, "It's ok, Sammy, I've got this."

Fixing him with a fierce glare, I make to argue and then almost pass out in shock as his mouth firmly lands on mine. His hands hold my face on either side and he kisses me deeply, which is an extremely pleasurable experience that makes my toes curl and my heart beat faster. I don't even care that psycho Jim has turned around to watch us like some kind of peep show and I'm still in shock when Marcus pulls back and hands Jim a £20 note. "Keep the change, mate, see you soon."

Before I can register what just happened, Marcus pulls me from the car and slams the door, almost making it fall off its hinges and pulls me at speed up the driveway to Valley House. "I'm sorry about that, Sammy, I could have asked him to drop us outside the front door but it's quicker this way."

I'm not arguing with him there and as he pulls me along at a brisk pace, I say breathlessly, "What was that all about? I thought I was paying."

"I know, but Jim would have asked for £5 and I always pay him more."

"Why?" I mean, we could have hired a car to get home for that and Marcus shrugs. "Times are hard. He lost a crop through disease and they had their subsidy cut. I know he's struggling, which is why he set up the cab business. It's not much but I like to help him out when I can."

My heart aches at his words because I suddenly see a side to him that I like – a lot. He may disguise his emotions at all times, but sometimes the caring side of him filters through the cracks and reveals a tantalising glimpse of an amazing person inside.

I feel so touched by his kindness; I am blinded by it.

As we head into Valley House, it suddenly strikes me that this night isn't over yet and this will be the biggest test of all.

The sleeping arrangements.

CHAPTER 14

We head in silence to Marcus's room, and suddenly the reality of my situation hits me. I will be sleeping in the same room, possibly the same bed, as this man who interests me way more than he would be comfortable with.

I need to play this cool and act unconcerned, but how? Just picturing the rather shabby nightwear I brought with me makes me howl inside because I expect he's used to women who dress in satin, silk and lace. Not fleecy pyjamas from Primark with Minnie mouse on them.

I feel as if I'm having another panic attack as he turns the handle to his room and we head inside and as he flicks on the light, the look in his eyes tells me he's enjoying this a little too much.

"So, here we are."

Running my tongue over my lips, I say in a rather high voice. "Yes, here we are."

He nods towards the bathroom and says airily, "You go first and I'll make a barricade, unless you want me to sleep on the floor."

"It's fine, a barricade's ok." I swallow nervously.

"We are adults and I'm sure we can make the best of a bad situation until my apartment is ready. When do you think that will be again?"

The fact he looks away, rings the alarm bells and rather than head off to the bathroom, I suddenly feel annoyed with it all. I've given up a lot to come here and the fact he's already changed the agreement doesn't sit well with me, so I say sharply, "I'm sorry, Marcus but you're not telling me something and I want to know what it is."

He looks up and I see the resignation in his eyes as he sighs. "The apartment isn't happening, Sammy. I'm sorry, it fell through."

"What do you mean, fell through, how?"

"There always was an apartment. It's just well. It's not built yet?"

"What?" I know he said it was behind, but this is unbelievable. It doesn't even have foundations and I am now seriously annoyed.

He sits on the bed and runs his fingers through his hair, which I've noticed he always seems to do when he's nervous.

"When the plans are agreed, and the inheritance is mine, I have included several apartments in the development. One of them has your name on the reservation, but we have to wait until then."

"But you said..." I drop down beside him with my head spinning and he says slightly guiltily, "I thought I could arrange one in town, but like I said, it fell through. The owner decided not to rent in the end because their plans changed. Then mum decided she wanted you both here and it would have looked odd if I'd argued against that. She still thinks we're deeply in love and I don't want to upset her."

"Why though? I mean, I get that you don't want to upset her because of your dad and all, but I'm sure she..."

"No, Sammy." Marcus frowns and I see his dark edge return as his eyes flash. "Mum needs to believe we're happy. It's all she wants for us. The dream. She believes in rainbows, fairy tales and happy endings because her own turned out so badly. The last thing she wants is a repeat of her own experience and so we all agreed to play our father at his own twisted game and spare our mothers feelings while we were at it."

"But what happens after two years? She will be upset then, when we part company and she feels the pain of your supposed break up. Surely that's not in her best interests."

Marcus looks like a wounded puppy as he stares at me for a long moment and then he says rather gruffly, "It may not even come to that."

My heart leaps inside me and I say with a whisper, "Why not?"

Shaking his head, he looks away and says abruptly, "We'll talk in the morning. It's late and we have an early start and a lot to do. If it helps, I'm sorry but there was nothing I could do."

He stands, leaving me staring after him with a hundred different thoughts running through my mind. What does he mean? Does he want this, hope it works maybe, or is he briefing Jim on a murder most foul because I wouldn't put anything past this man. One thing's certain, though, Marcus Hudson is a man of secrets and closed emotions. Sometimes they make it through that dark mind of his and reveal an actual human inside, but they are quickly pulled back when he is challenged and has to explain them.

~

AFTER I SHOWER and change for bed, I venture back into the room and note it's empty and I'm a little relieved about that.

Maybe he's had second thoughts and decided to sleep elsewhere and so I curl up in his huge bed that he has stuffed pillows down the centre of and just enjoy the fact I'm alone at last and safely tucked up in bed.

My eyes close almost before my head hits the pillow and if he joins me, I don't register it because the next thing I know, the warm sun is kissing me awake as the morning pushes the night away.

For a moment I think I'm back at my flat, but as I stretch and open my eyes, the unfamiliar wallpaper reminds me what happened yesterday.

Quickly, I look to my left and see the empty space and my heart thumps, either with relief or disappointment, that I'm alone.

Bleary eyed, I sit up and take a closer look and note the indentation on the pillow revealing somebody slept on it at least and then as the door to the bathroom opens and Marcus heads inside with just a towel slung around his waist, my mouth drops open with a mixture of shock and desire.

"Morning, angel, how did you sleep?"

"On my back, I think?"

He snorts. "I mean, did you sleep? It can be difficult the first night in a strange bed."

"I did as it happens." Smiling shyly, I try to rake my fingers through my hair because I am so embarrassed at how I must look in his eyes. Feeling the tangles, I'm sure he must be sighing inside because this man is never anything but perfect in his appearance, his surroundings and his outlook. There is never anything out of place. I got that from the orderly cabin he had on the cruise ship and his room is no different. Marcus likes everything just so, and seeing the hot mess in his bed must be giving him anxiety.

Feeling out of my league, I say quickly, "Well, if you've finished, I should freshen up."

He nods and I leap out of the bed and make a dive for the bathroom door before he can register that my bottoms don't match my top, that is also frayed at the edges.

Leaning back against the locked door, I try to get my head around the situation I'm in. I must be mad. It all seemed like such a good idea on the cruise. The cocktails are probably to blame for that rash decision, but now I'm coming down to earth with a bang. I went to bed with a stranger who I agreed to marry. This is insane, and it's no wonder I didn't want my parents to know. It's like one of those trashy reality programmes. Married at First Sight or something along those lines and my heart beats out of control when I picture their faces when I tell them what I've done.

They must never find out. I told them I was starting a new job in a new town and that's all they need to know. If it works out, I'll make something up to make me look better and if it doesn't, they will never know what a mistake I made with my life.

My parent's opinion matters to me – a lot and just imagining how hurt they will be makes me want to weep tears of self-loathing. Why am I such a mess?

CHAPTER 15

Camilla is sitting at the dining table when we head down to breakfast and smiles as we join her. "Darlings, this is so nice. Breakfast as a family."

"Where is everyone?" Marcus pulls out a chair for me and as his fingers brush my neck, a delicious shiver passes through me.

"Jake and Florrie are still in bed and I'm guessing that will happen a lot." I feel my skin heating as she winks suggestively and throws a look at her son, who is frowning at something on his phone. "Dom left early and Brad didn't come home last night."

She giggles and says with a whisper, "Mind you, I nearly didn't make it myself. What a night."

Remembering her date, I lean forward and say with interest. "Tell me about your evening. What was he like?"

Marcus huffs beside me and Camilla giggles. "Gorgeous, darling, absolutely gorgeous, but way too young for me. It was like being on a date with my son."

"For god's sake mum, really." Marcus looks slightly nauseous and I share an amused grin with his mother.

"Well..." She leans closer. "Irene's date was her regular, Ian. A nice man, around thirty I think, who is a gas engineer by day and a playboy at night."

Briefly, I wonder if I should mention this to Jim. It may pay more than being a taxi service, it could work.

Camilla continues, "Anyway, Richie was my date, and he works at the sports centre in Riverton as a lifeguard. So fit darling and I wouldn't say no to the kiss of life from him."

"Mother, please, I haven't eaten yet."

Marcus sighs, which makes us giggle even more, and as he catches my eye, I'm surprised at the sweet smile he gives me before turning back to his phone.

"So, anyway, Richie asked if I would give him good feedback for his reviews, you know, like Trip Advisor and I was happy to give him five stars, obviously. However, I've decided to go for someone a little older next time because it drew a few raised eyebrows in my direction and I think it would look better if the man was more my age."

"Sounds like a good plan." Marcus doesn't even look up but is obviously listening to every word she speaks and I wonder how he can multi task in this way when normally men just aren't that good at it.

"So, what happens now?" I am so interested in Camilla's love life, even more than my own, and she leans back and picks up her phone. "Well, I've completed my profile and will spend the morning swiping for potentials. I may get Alexis to help me, I'm sure she wouldn't mind."

"Alexa, mum and she's a microchip for god's sake, not your friend."

"There's no need to be brusque, darling, it doesn't suit you."

She starts to eat her bowl of Greek yoghurt and muesli and I wonder if I should offer to cook something for Marcus, who is just sipping orange juice and looking distracted. "So, um, would you like some toast or something?"

Marcus looks up in surprise, and Camilla laughs. "Darling, we don't make our own breakfast here. Mrs Jenkins will be in soon with my full English. Just place your order with her."

"Mrs Jenkins?"

"Our housekeeper. She comes in early and makes breakfast, does some cleaning and then leaves us to it. Such a godsend really, and one of my most valued friends. I don't know what we would do without Mrs Jenkins."

As if on cue, a small woman heads into the room with wispy grey hair escaping from a messy bun and a flowery apron that covers her bright pink dress. She looks at me with a kind smile and says, "You must be Sammy, lovely to meet you."

I can't help but like her on sight and smile. "Me too."

"So, dear, this is how it works. Cereal is on the side and juice and I'll fetch you a tea or coffee and some toast. I can also fix you eggs, bacon, pancakes, anything hot, really. Marcus usually likes an omelette on Tuesdays, but I can do you something else if you like."

I stare at her in astonishment because surely people don't really live like this. It's all a little surreal and I feel bad asking, so just say with a nervous laugh, "Oh, toast will be fine."

"Add some bacon, poached eggs, and a grilled tomato. Granary bread for the toast with half fat butter."

Marcus doesn't even look up from his phone and just rattles off the request without blinking and as I open my mouth to speak, Camilla says quickly, "Just humour him, darling. Leave what you can't eat and I'll feed it to the chickens."

Mrs Jenkins nods in agreement and heads off and I turn to Marcus and hiss, "I can order my own breakfast."

"No, you can't."

I stare at him in shock as he lowers his phone and leans back with a smirk.

"You were being polite. You felt awkward asking someone to make you food you think you should prepare yourself. You are hungry and need something to keep you going because this day promises to be manic. I stepped in to save you from yourself and I will not apologise for that. Get used to it, Sammy, because I am here to make your life easier."

"But I only wanted toast. I don't eat breakfast."

"Good god, Sammy, breakfast is the most important meal of the day." Camilla shakes her head and shares a look with her son. "Tell her, Marcus. It's our family tradition. We all eat breakfast together and make it count. Then we can face the day knowing we are prepared for what that will bring. I mean, what if you can't make lunch and have important meetings that get in the way of that? What if dinner is delayed? You will be fading away before the day is through. No, we insist on a full and hearty breakfast because it's important to your body and Marcus is right, sometimes you just need someone to guide you down the right path."

Camilla looks so fierce it shocks me a little and I see a lot of her son in her eyes as she lays down the law.

Marcus is obviously disinterested in the whole conversation and so I lean back and sip on my juice, wondering when my life got so mad.

Luckily, Florrie and Jake soon join us and I watch a virtually identical lecture when she opts for cereal and refuses the whole cooked breakfast thing and yet as soon as mine arrives, I'm grateful for the intervention because I cannot eat this fast enough, it is that good.

Florrie leans across while Camilla chats to Jake and whispers, "This place is something else, I'm pinching myself right now."

She frowns and then looks across at Marcus and whispers, "How was it, you know, sleeping with him?"

"I couldn't tell you. I fell asleep alone and woke up alone."

She grins and I see the light dancing in her eyes as she looks at Jake. "Well, I'm pleased to report I'm happy with our rash decision. I knew he was the man for me."

Seeing the wink he directs her way and the lust bridling in his eyes once again, I feel envious of my lucky friend as Marcus frowns at something on his phone. Sighing inside, I wonder if this is it with him. A snapshot of my future if things did work out after all.

Watching everyone around the table, I feel welcome here but still feel on the edge. It's obvious Jake and Florrie were made for each other. They fell into an easy relationship on the cruise that is only building momentum with every hour they're together. Even Camilla is finding herself and yet Marcus, well, I'm still not sure what to make of him. I lust after him, like him even, but I'm not sure I trust him and that is worrying me more than the hole I appear to have fallen head first into with no way out.

CHAPTER 16

Marcus's office is in Dream Valley town, a short distance from the Cosy Kettle. It sits above a convenience store called Valley Marketplace and it's got a great view of the street outside.

I look around and smile to myself as I see everything neatly in its place. The interior is minimal but practical and the neat filing cabinets are new and gleaming and the two desks that sit side by side are orderly and clean.

There is not a piece of paper out of place and I stare at the man responsible for that as he surveys his kingdom looking like a well-heeled king.

Dressed in a black suit with a white shirt, his pink tie matching my own pale pink shift dress. Knowing him, it's deliberate because he dressed after me this morning and colour coordinating outfits is something I wouldn't put past him.

He looks like a successful man and I suppose he is. He has it all worked out except for one vital ingredient. He needs the land to make it all happen.

"Your desk is there, Sammy. I have the passwords for the

computer written on the first page of the notebook in the top drawer. There is also a list of jobs that need to be completed by the close of business and after that we have an appointment with Harrison Bowers, the local vicar.

My nerves are out of control as my situation hits home. This is it. I'm here and preparing to honour my side of the bargain.

Marcus heads for his desk and removes his jacket, before hanging it on a hanger on a hook on the wall. He says quickly, "You can keep your bag in the bottom drawer. It has a combination lock, so should be safe."

"From who?"

There is nobody here but us, and he shrugs. "Just in case. Crime is low in Dream Valley, but you can't rule it out. It only takes someone to distract you and they could be off with your bag before you even know it."

Doubting that would ever happen here, I do as he says anyway and sit down, feeling quite important for once in my life.

Marcus is soon tapping away on his computer and so I look at the list of things to do for today and read through it with interest.

1. 9 am Check emails.

2. 9.15 am Check answerphone and return calls.

3. 9.30 am Deal with queries.

4. 10.30 am Collect coffee order from the Cosy Kettle.

5. 11.00 am Call expressions of interest from folder on desktop. Check their current position.

6. 12 pm Research.

7. 1-1.30 Lunch at The Olive Tree.

8. 1.30 -2 pm Check emails and answerphone and return calls.

9. 2 pm Meeting with Elspeth Grainger (Take minutes)

10. 3 pm Meeting with Connor Smith (Take notes)

11. 4 pm Fetch coffee order from Cosy Kettle.
12. 4.30 pm Check out opposition.
13. 5.30 pm Draw up the list for the next day.
14. 6 pm Tidy office, leave for meeting with vicar.

I stare at it in surprise and say quickly, "Did you do this?"

"Yes, is there a problem?"

"It's just so…"

"Structured." He looks across at me sharply and I nod. "Yes, it is. Do I have to stick to the times, or can I just follow it at my own pace?"

"Stick to the plan, Sammy."

As he looks away, I wonder if this is how he lives his life. By numbers, bullet points, and action plans.

Then I hear him say sharply, "It's 9.15 already, Sammy, you're falling behind."

I stare at him in shock but he doesn't even look my way and feeling quite hot already, I quickly grasp the password list and fire up the computer.

Everything I can possibly need is documented in this book. Addresses, telephone numbers, passwords, all neatly written under headings and separated by dividers. He must have spent hours on this, and I'm guessing there is not a single thing left undone. The man's a machine and I'm the fool who agreed to marry him.

Once I manage to navigate my way to the company email, I stare in shock at the total of unread ones. 250! I'm already past that point in my list and should be on answerphone messages and returning calls by now. I'm almost tempted to group delete the lot of them but instead I press the answerphone and quickly grab my pen and list down the various messages that don't appear to end.

By the time my pen runs out of steam, I only have forty minutes to deal with it all and I feel slightly nervous about that as I prepare to call back the people who want to register their interest. I wonder what they are registering because Dream Valley hasn't had the development approved as far as I know.

"Um, Marcus?"

His head snaps up and his frown tells me I've interrupted his concentration and I say nervously, "What am I supposed to tell them exactly?"

"About what?"

"The development, it's just that we have no dates, no brochures, no nothing actually. What if you don't get the land, isn't this all rather, well, a waste of time?"

He leans back in his seat and I feel like a naughty child before the headmaster as he taps his pen on the desk and shakes his head. "I have other developments, Sammy."

"I'm sorry." Now I'm confused, and a cocky smirk tugs at his lips as he enjoys my reaction.

"Dream Valley is just one of them. There's the one in Riverton, two actually. The details are filed on your desktop in the relevant folders. I am also in negotiations with a builder in Cronton and another one in Hansley Dale. You see, I manage the sales of many local builders. The marketing, the sales, and the aftercare. Dream Valley is one hundred per cent my own, but the land I manage is usually owned by somebody else. This is my business, Sammy, estate management and Dream Valley is just one of many. A very important one, but not the only one. I thought you knew that."

Feeling like a fool, I nod and turn my attention to the desktop as Marcus says firmly, "Don't fall behind on your list. Playing catch up is not good for business."

Feeling like a fish out of water, I genuinely hate him right now after he threw me back right into the deep end. Where is the staff training in this place and if he's that busy, why is he working alone? I am actually fuming right now and just suck it up and struggle through, until he says abruptly, "It's 10. 30, Sammy, shouldn't you be leaving already."

Jumping up, I look at the next item on my list and am relieved to see I get to escape for a while and hesitate by the door, not knowing if I should interrupt or not.

"Spit it out."

His voice is firm and I wonder where the man I met last night lives during the day because this guy is seriously pissing me off.

"Do you have petty cash, or shall I just pay."

"We have an account, there's no need for money."

"Oh, and um, what do you want exactly?"

"They have my order, just add yours to it and they will have it ready when you call."

Saying nothing else, I head outside, just grateful to escape for a while because working with Marcus Hudson is like stepping into the fire and getting badly burned.

CHAPTER 17

I feel relieved when I head into the Cosy Kettle and note that Laura isn't working today and in her place is a woman who looks up and smiles from behind the counter.

"Can I help you?"

"Yes, I believe you have an order for Marcus Hudson."

She looks interested and I can feel her looking me up and down as she judges me. It feels slightly uncomfortable as I wait for her expression to change, but she just nods and says sweetly, "So, I need to add your order to the daily requirements. What do you like?"

"A latte please, um…"

"Miranda Constable. Proprietor and general dogsbody."

She tucks a stray hair behind her ear and looks so kind I like her on sight.

"So…" She turns and starts assembling our drinks as she speaks. "You must be Marcus's fiancée, Laura told me you were in yesterday."

"Yes, although between me and you, Miranda, I'm not really sure about the living and working together thing."

If I feel bad about talking about him behind his back, Miranda doesn't seem to care and snorts. "Rather you than me, dear. I mean, he may look like a film star but his OCD would drive me crazy."

She looks up and winks. "Sometimes for fun, I mess with his mind and serve his coffee in a paper cup instead of his usual china one to go."

She holds up one of those travel mugs that must be his and winks. "It drives him crazy. He hates those disposable ones, probably because his mum is so into green living these days and it's rubbed off on him, but I love prodding the beast, just don't tell him it's deliberate."

Laughing, I decide she is now my new best friend because anyone who prods the beast as she says, gets my full support because you can't plan everything in life down to the colour of your freaking tie and I should take a leaf out of her book and shake things up a little.

She looks at me with interest. "So, the wedding. I must say the town is buzzing about that."

"It is?" I'm surprised, and she smiles. "We've watched those lads grow up and listened to the gossip they provide us with on a daily basis. The fact some lucky lady has managed to snare the biggest beast of all is breaking news around here. I mean, way to go honey, you've scored a bullseye with him."

Feeling a little uncomfortable, I shift on the spot as she chatters on. "I'm guessing you are public enemy number one among the single women it this place because there have been many eyes made at Marcus Hudson. Sometimes he even sees them and they get all hopeful for a while, but that's soon knocked out of them when he refuses their calls and moves onto the next willing applicant."

I'm sure she's only being friendly, but I'm not enjoying this conversation because the thought of Marcus sweeping through the willing women of Dream Valley doesn't paint a nice picture at all.

After a while, she checks herself and says with a hint of an apology in her voice. "Anyway, that's all history now because he met his match. He's a lucky man, dear, and don't let anyone tell you differently. Him included."

Handing me the two coffees, she smiles and says quickly, "Wait."

She lifts the lid off a glass jar on the counter and slips two shortbreads into a paper bag. "Here, a little welcome gift from me to you. It's lovely to meet you and please forgive my gossiping. I'm known for it and I forget that not everybody knows that."

My heart lifts with this one small act of kindness and I smile. "Thank you, that's such a lovely thing to do."

As I head back the way I came, I feel better about this place now. Maybe not everybody hates the new girl in town, which gives me a little hope, at least.

∼

MARCUS LOOKS up as I head inside, balancing the coffees and smiles. "I need this."

Handing it to him, I try to maintain professional indifference when we're here because I can't seem to stop lusting after this man at every opportunity.

He takes a sip and fixes me with his soul shattering gaze. "How has your morning been so far? Are you finding everything you need?"

"Yes thanks."

I turn my attention to my work, effectively cutting him off because, quite honestly, I feel annoyed. He has just expected me to get on with it without showing me a thing and then speaking to me like I'm an idiot when I ask questions. A little piece of my heart is hardening against Marcus Hudson because of it, and I need to remember he is paying me to do two jobs and I must keep any familiarity firmly out of the workplace.

I can feel him watching me and is probably surprised at how cool I am, but I couldn't care less. He deserves to feel the effects of his own disinterest and it is giving me great pleasure in dishing some right back at him.

As I pick up the phone, I intend on calling every expression of interest on the list in the allotted time and am surprised when a strong hand takes the phone from me and I hear a soft, "I'm sorry, angel."

Looking up, I think my expression must tell a thousand words because he shakes his head and says softly, "You're angry with me and I don't blame you for that."

He reaches out and lifts a strand of my hair and twists it in his hands, and I'm surprised by the look in his eyes as he stares into mine. There's something about Marcus that I just can't put my finger on. Something he's holding back and keeping well hidden. Sometimes he seems so cold and indifferent, it makes me feel used. Then there are times like this that he makes me feel like the most important person in his life.

"Scrap the list today. Just take it at your own pace."

"Why?" I feel as if I've failed already and he shrugs. "I'm not being fair on you. I'm expecting you to know everything immediately and I'm an idiot for expecting so much."

He couldn't hurt me anymore if he tried because I don't want favours; for him to make excuses for me, even though he is solely to blame for it, anyway.

Leaning away from his hand, I shrug and turn my attention to the screen and say airily, "I have a job to do. I've got to learn it somehow, so it may as well be treading water in the deep end."

I completely blank him out because he is so conflicting. I hate that he can turn on the charm and I forgive him everything. That he just has to mess with my mind a little and I'm over it already. Miranda's story just made me harden my heart a little as I picture him manipulating the local girls to suit his own agenda. Well, I have made my bed but I can mess it up a bit if I want and so I say coolly, "Anyway, I prefer to learn by actions rather than words, so if you don't mind, I have a schedule to follow."

He takes the hint - luckily and returns to his own work and I'm surprised when he says loudly, "Lunch time."

I look up and note it's 1.30 already and say quickly, "It's ok, I can work through."

He shakes his head and says firmly, "No, I don't eat alone."

Then he reaches for my hand and I have no choice but to take it and follow him to the door feeling like the hired help again. *I don't eat alone.* I bet you don't and I imagine there is a line of girls waiting for the invitation. I'm starting to see just what I've agreed to here because when Marcus says jump, it appears the whole town jumps in unison.

My heart sinks when we head to the Olive Tree and I wonder why a quick sandwich wouldn't suffice because I'm not sure I can face anything more if I'm honest.

Maria meets us at the door and runs her sharp gaze over me, dismissing me out of hand, and smiles seductively at Marcus, making me roll my eyes. This is getting so old already and I am itching to change the record.

"So, we met again."

She purrs up at him and I wonder what she means by that. The look she throws at me is a triumphant one and I wonder when that could have been because to my knowledge, he's been by my side the whole time. Then an icy feeling washes over me as I remember falling asleep and wonder if somehow, he snuck out for a booty call with this woman – I wouldn't put it past him and her, actually. I expect he made the call, and they met under a tree, or against it probably. She's just the type to answer the call of the wild and turn up, ready for action at the slightest nod and a wink.

The more I think about it, the more my vivid imagination takes over and soon I have them starring in an x-rated movie that wins awards in the porn world. Just imagining this hussy anywhere near him makes my blood boil and revenge to blacken my heart. Apparently, he is unaware of the storm brewing because he just follows her to the table and expects me to follow.

Instead, I turn and walk toward the ladies because I am feeling like throwing up, anyway.

I actually hate myself right now and as I run some water over my hands, I look in the mirror and see jealousy looking back at me. I hate that he affects me and I hate that I want him. I hate the situation I'm in too because he has all the control. I am so busy trying to make him love me, I am not loving myself and I despise the person I'm becoming.

I wish I could stay in here all day but know I must head back and put up with more of it and sighing, I make a vow to myself to protect my heart at all costs, even if it means erecting a quick wall around it and reinforcing it with barbed wire.

CHAPTER 18

Somehow, I manage to get through lunch and number eight on my list before our meeting with Elspeth Grainger, the head of the planning committee in Riverton.

Marcus quickly briefed me on what to expect and as she breezes into the office, I'm struck by her commanding presence almost immediately.

"Marcus." She extends her hand and shakes his vigorously before turning to me and handing me her coat.

"Take care of that for me and fetch me a glass of water fresh from the tap."

Marcus looks angry on my behalf but I say quickly, "Of course."

Rushing over to the cooler, I fill a cup with water after hanging her coat on the peg behind the door.

Then, as she snatches it from my hand and guzzles it down, I take a moment to grab my notebook and try to blend into the shadows in the corner of the room.

"Marcus, you have exactly ten minutes before I need to fly."

Picturing her broomstick waiting in the air outside, gives me a moment's pleasure, along with the realisation that I only need to spend ten minutes in her company taking notes.

"Speak." She fixes him with a forceful look and I almost feel sorry for him as he says quickly, "I wanted to pick your brains about the time limits involved if I get the plans approved for Dream Valley Heights."

She looks interested. "Do you have the land?"

"I soon will."

"Then call me again when you have. I don't deal with what ifs and maybes, Mr Hudson, I deal with facts and until you are the legitimate owner of the land you seek planning permission for, there is no point in our conversation."

She looks at him so fiercely I hold my breath and Marcus looks resigned to getting absolutely nowhere with her today, anyway.

She stands and holds out her hand as if her coat will magically transport itself from the peg by the door and I marvel at a woman who expects everything done for her. I wouldn't be surprised if she does have a broomstick waiting as she prepares to fly off and curse some other unfortunate soul.

Quickly, I scramble to my feet and dive for the coat and as I almost trip over my feet to deliver it, she snatches it from my hand without a glance in my direction.

Then she turns and leaves without another word, despite the fact Marcus tries to shake her hand and thank her for coming.

As the door slams behind her, I look at him in horror as he shrugs. "That went better than I expected."

"Seriously, what constitutes going badly, then?"

I shake my head as his mouth twitches, and I look at him in shock. Is he finding this funny?

"That woman is something else."

He sits down and groans. "There's a reason she heads up the planning committee because nobody would dare upset her. She is ferocious, a beast, and a woman who takes no prisoners but she's fair and usually right."

"If you knew all this, why did you bring her here knowing what she's like. She could be angry that you wasted her time."

Wandering across, I perch on the edge of his desk and watch his eyes narrow as he sees that I've creased one of his papers. Feeling a little devilish, I sweep my arm down and knock a pile to the floor, and his eyes glitter as I test his immaculate resolve.

"Oops, sorry."

Grinning, I lean down and grab the papers and just toss them in a heap on his desk and grin at the expression in his eyes as he struggles to deal with the disorder.

"What's the matter?"

I act innocent, and he looks up and shrugs. "Nothing."

I know he would never admit that he has a thing about mess and the fact I'm even on his desk is probably giving him anxiety.

"So, the permission you need, I'm guessing that comes after we marry."

"Yes, it will only take a signature and then the plans are ready to submit to the council."

Feeling all powerful right now, I realise I have Marcus Hudson in the palm of my hand and I study my nails with disinterest.

"So, what happens if we say, don't get married for some reason? What happens then?"

I swear the tension in the room increases as he faces the possibility he may not be in control after all and he looks so tense I stare at him with interest, wondering how far I should go with this. The thing is, after the morning I've had, I want to see a little of his control slip away. He has been cool, rather abrupt and made me feel incompetent. Then Maria smiled up at him and it made my blood boil. Miranda coloured in a few lines too with her descriptions of how the Hudson brothers run rings around the women of this town and I suppose it's all added up to a very bad case of pissed off.

He looks at me sharply, "Is there a reason you can think of?"

He stares at me long and hard and I shrug. "Maybe."

"Will you tell me about it?"

His voice is ringed with a hard edge and I swing my legs against his desk, the dull thud of my shoe adding a beat of tension in the room that really isn't needed.

Sighing, I look him straight in the eye and say coolly. "Well, firstly you promised me an apartment and then didn't deliver. Secondly, I appear to be the most hated woman in Dream Valley right now which makes me wonder if this is the place for me and thirdly, I'm not sure if this is the right thing, anyway because I can't bear the thought of tearing up the countryside for 'progression' as you call it. Maybe Dom's right to want to preserve it."

Marcus looks so shaken I immediately feel bad as his usual cool mask slips a little.

I can tell he's not used to this, somebody going against his carefully laid plans and probably expected that I would fall into line just by a whiff of his aftershave.

He needs to know that he has to work at life and not everything will fall into his lap and even though I don't really have doubts, I want him to think I have.

"You want an apartment then."

I'm surprised at the vulnerable look in his eye as he looks almost disappointed, and it throws me a little.

"Well, you did promise."

"Which I will keep. I told you, one of the new ones has

your name on it already and I fully intend on putting it in your name if all goes according to plan."

"Oh." I stare at him with a mixture of shock and strangely disappointment because if he is gifting me an apartment, it's payment for my part of the deal, meaning that's all this is to him – a deal. He still intends on marrying me and then palming me off two years later with a handshake and a place to live.

I'm not sure why that disappoints me so much. Surely that was the deal, after all. But it doesn't make me feel good about myself because I'm not in it for the money. I'm in this for him.

Feeling a little cheap and unworthy, I fight my emotions and slip off the desk and he says quickly, "What's on your mind?"

"Nothing." I turn away because I don't want to look at him anymore, in case I don't like what I see in his eyes. I want him to look at me like Jake does Florrie. He just finds his phone more interesting and I wonder if he's more like his father than I'd like because from the sounds of it, this was Camilla's life, which makes me wonder if I should bother to try. I don't want that; I want the dream. My own version of Prince Charming, and it's doubtful I will find that here. But I want it to be him so badly it's blinding me to reality.

I feel like such a fool and head back to my desk as he says behind me, "Sammy Jo."

Sinking wearily into my seat, I detect a hint of panic in his voice and know it's because his beloved dream has been threatened. But so has mine, because I'm fast coming to the conclusion that Marcus is all about the business and nothing else. I'm a means to an end; a willing fool with just a sense of adventure and a little fairy dust in her eye. He doesn't want me and he never did, and I have to suck that up and decide whether this is worth my integrity or not.

Grabbing the phone, I cut him off by calling some potential customers and I can tell he's angry about that, but I couldn't care less. I'm in self-preservation mode right now and need to formulate a plan because one thing's for sure, Marcus's plans only involve his dreams and he will make them happen, regardless of anyone who stands in his way.

CHAPTER 19

For the rest of the day, I threw myself into work and every time Marcus tried to engage me in conversation; I dodged it. I know he's worried about my apparent change of heart and part of me wants to reassure him, but I need to work out what's going on here. I'm not sure if he even thinks of me in any other way than somebody who stands between him and his dream, and I don't like how that makes me feel. For the first time since I agreed to this, I almost long for my uncomplicated life in my rented flat, working on the production line at Hainseys electrical.

I've never been a girl who found life easy. I've always put on a brave face and made out I wanted to be free to live my best life – but I don't. I want the family and the person who looks at me with stardust in his eyes. Somebody who fights for me and has my back at all times. A man who adores me and I adore him, a team, a family unit and I'm not even that bothered about money. That's just something we need to live, not exist. I would pack everything up in a tent and set off travelling if I found the right man to walk by my side.

Just picturing Marcus dirtying his hands and putting up a

tent makes me smile, and I wasn't even aware I was doing it until I hear a soft, "What are you thinking?"

Looking up, I see Marcus watching me with a smile on his face and for a moment our eyes connect and the level of intimacy that brings makes my heart beat a little faster.

"You, in a tent actually."

The horror in his eyes makes me giggle and lightens the previously tense atmosphere instantaneously.

"Why?" He looks confused, and I shrug. "Why not? People go camping, I wondered if it's something you like to do."

"You want to go camping." The sigh that accompanies his words makes me giggle as he dreads being placed firmly out of his comfort zone, and I laugh. "Relax, I don't mean I want to go, I was just thinking…well, it's silly really."

"Tell me."

His voice is soft and curious and for some reason my heart softens again and I lean forward and deliver words I'm sure should have stayed well-guarded.

"I was thinking about Jake and Florrie. The way he looks at her tells me he's smitten. He would do anything for her and I know she feels the same way, which made me think about my own situation."

I hesitate because this could shut the lid on the can of what's happening here and I sigh heavily. "Don't you want that too, Marcus? To be so wrapped up in the person you're dating that you would agree to anything just to make them happy. Even putting yourself out of your comfort zone because it's something they want?"

He remains silent, which tells me I should follow suit, but I can't. "You see, I've never had that. I've never been the most important person in any man's life unless you count my dad."

I feel a pang when I think about my dad and what he would think if he knew what I was planning.

"It just makes me feel bad that I'm selling myself short. In helping you, I help myself, financially speaking but that doesn't feel right to me. I want to earn money, of course I do, but through hard work, not this. There are too many people involved. Your mother, for one. I hate deceiving her and I can't even call my own parents in case I blurt it all out somehow. Florrie and Jake know, and your brothers, but I know they think badly of me. Then there's you."

"Me?" He sounds shocked and who can blame him. I'm acting like a hysterical idiot right now and he must be wondering what he's agreed to.

"Yes, Marcus, you."

A knock on the door makes us jump and Marcus groans. "Connor."

Jumping up, I put on my brave face and shrug. "It's fine, it wasn't important, anyway."

As I head off to greet our next guest, I try to regain my composure. I can't let Marcus in because it's obvious he's not on the same page as me and I should take a long, hard look at this situation before I dig myself any deeper into it.

∽

BY THE END of the day, I'm so tired all I want to do is head back to Valley House and take a long, deep bath, filled with essential oils that relax the soul. Marcus was quiet and a little distant for the rest of the afternoon and I just threw myself into my work as a means to escape and to prove that I can do this. I will be strong and see this through because I'm a woman of my word, but at what cost to my heart?

We don't even have time to go back to the house because apparently, we have a meeting with the vicar on the way home.

∽

St Thomas's church is a sweet country place of worship that lifts the spirits of the living and provides a haven for those who don't. I love the way it rests at the heart of the valley, the surrounding fields nestling against its stone walls like a cosy blanket. The graveyard is well tended, with a cobbled path that winds its way through the gravestones, with ageing benches labelled with copper plaques, reminding us of deceased locals who apparently loved this place. The oak door under the gothic arch beckons a weary parishioner through its holy doors, and I imagine a garland of flowers framing it on what will be my wedding day. In fact, as churches go, this one would be in my top ten; not that I make a habit of grading places of worship but worthy of a photo and inclusion on Camilla's Pinterest board.

As we edge our way inside, I stare around in hushed awe at the ancient building with centuries of worship and important events surrounding me. I can almost see the people through the ages who have seen this same view. Gathering together in good and hard times to take comfort in religion and the company of like-minded neighbours and friends. The gleaming polished pews and tapestry kneelers stand patiently waiting for worship and the beautiful stained-glass windows gleam as the retreating sun shines through the cracks.

Marcus shivers beside me and I wonder if the devil in him is uncomfortable right now because seeing Marcus grace this church with his presence is like watching judgement day. He looks so out of place here with his angry scowl and flashing eyes, and I half expect him to be struck down at the altar as God punishes the devil within.

Almost as soon as we enter, a man heads our way and judging by the fact he's wearing the uniform of God's faithful servant, I'd say he was Harrison Bowers, the vicar.

He looks pleasant enough and pushes his glasses further

up his nose as he peers through them with screwed-up eyes, making me wonder if they are fit for purpose. Then he says in the loudest voice I have heard in my life, "MARCUS and you must be Sammy, welcome, welcome, don't stand on ceremony and come closer and let me look at you."

Marcus quickly shoves me forward, and as I stumble, I reach out and steady myself on the pew, turning to glare at him with an irritated frown.

He just shrugs and looks away and I wonder what he's thinking because for some reason he's been edgy since our conversation earlier on today.

"Take a seat people and let's talk about the happy day."

Marcus sits beside me, but he may as well be in another church because I can tell his mind is wandering already, which makes my heart sink. The fact he can't look at his phone is of no consequence because he just stares around him with an air of boredom that tears at my heart.

"So, Sammy Jo, isn't it, or do you have a different birth name?"

"Yes, Samantha Josephine um…"

"Go on." Harrison looks up from his note-taking and my cheeks burn as I say, "Hermione."

Marcus looks at me in surprise and I laugh nervously. "My grandmother's name. I know it's a bit of a mouthful, so now you know why I shortened it."

"A beautiful name for a beautiful girl." Harrison's voice booms out and I wonder if he can talk in anything but full volume. His voice bounces around us like the town crier and I expect it's because he's used to shouting so they can hear at the back.

"And Marcus…" He looks at Marcus, his pen poised and Marcus says tightly, "Marcus Sheridan Hudson."

I struggle to stop myself from bursting into laughter, and

the warning look he gives me tells me he's not amused by my reaction.

"SO." I jump as Harrison's voice booms in my ear, "The Service. Any hymn choices?"

Marcus shakes his head as my heart sinks. Feeling as if one of us should show some interest, at least, I say, "Well…"

Harrison interrupts, "Unless it's Onward Christian Soldiers, Jerusalem, or All Things Bright and Beautiful, you may as well not bother."

He looks around him and says in an almost normal voice, which he obviously thinks is a whisper, "Mrs Judd only knows them. Anything else and she won't sleep for a week. You see, she'll be up all night on YouTube practising them and won't get any sleep. Then she'll panic and miss a few notes and end up playing what she knows, anyway. Trust me, it's best to go with me on this one."

Marcus shrugs, "Fine by me."

"Can we provide our own pianist then?"

I glare at Marcus because he is seriously annoying me now, and Harrison shakes his head. "You can, of course, but they wouldn't be insured and you would need to take that out yourselves."

"Insured, why?"

Looking around me, I wonder if God would strike down an unauthorised organist in the church and Harrison shrugs. "Church rules to protect their staff."

Wow, it's like a holy union of a different kind and if it wasn't so personal, I'd be impressed. Sighing, I nod. "Onward Christian Soldiers it is then."

"Unless you intend on a Christmas wedding of course." Harrison looks thoughtful. "She can also do, Away in a Manger and Ding Dong Merrily on High."

Marcus starts to laugh and I elbow him sharply in the ribs

and say with an edge to my voice, "No, the usual selection will be fine."

"SO..." I jump as he shouts in my ear, "SEX."

I stare at him in utter shock as Marcus sits up, now more than interested in what's happening.

"I'm sorry." My voice sounds weak and rather beaten as Harrison fixes us with a gleam in his eye and says for the whole world to hear. "Sex before marriage. Have you had any?"

I want that bolt of lightning to strike me down already because what the hell is going on – if I can say that word here, that is? Marcus apparently has no shame because he shrugs and says, "I have."

Harrison doesn't look surprised about that and turns his attention to me with interest. "What about you?"

Marcus is enjoying this as I struggle with my conscience because if I lie, I won't go to Heaven and if I admit to it, I probably won't either because there are probably rules on that too.

Luckily, Marcus comes to my rescue and says firmly, "I fail to see what this has to do with our wedding. Surely that's private information."

Harrison shrugs. "I need to have the sex talk. If you've already had it, we can skip that part, sorry church rules."

Just imagining the sex talk with this man makes me blurt out, "We can skip that part."

They both look at me and I feel my cheeks burning as my soul goes down in flames. I would say 'up' but my destination is definitely down and I have never felt so cheap in my life, although slightly relieved to dodge the sex talk bullet.

Harrison notes something down and I wonder if it's a black mark against my name that he will email to God later. This whole experience is excruciating made all the worse by Marcus's apparent disinterest in the whole thing.

"VOWS." I look up and Harrison says with a smile, "The most important part of any service and you can either go with the old version or the new."

"What do you think, Marcus?" I am determined to drag him into this and have an actual opinion on our wedding and he surprises me by saying, "I have written my own."

Of course he has. He has probably crafted a contract of the most unromantic kind that he will probably expect me to sign and get witnessed three times. A prenup, a get out of marriage free card and a surrender of all his responsibilities where it concerns me.

"And you?" Harrison turns his attention to me and I look at Marcus as if he has all the answers, but all I see is a slightly curious stare as I shrug. "I can write mine too if you like."

"It doesn't matter to me; the ones God has provided are good enough, but some modern people like to flout the church's rule book and think they know best."

The fact he disapproves makes up my mind and I smile. "I'll write my own."

The slight smile on Marcus's face tells me he approves of my decision and just for one moment, we agree on something.

Once again, Harrison makes some notes and I already know I now have two strikes against me.

"BRIDAL PARTY! How many?"

Once again, I look at Marcus for guidance because I'm drowning here.

"I have three best men who will double as ushers."

As expected, he is straight to the point and all eyes turn to me and I say quickly, "One bridesmaid."

"Then we will meet tomorrow evening for the rehearsal because time is of the essence here, apparently."

Why do I imagine he looks at my stomach and why am I already heated about that possibility? Sex. Procreation and wedding vows are crowding my mind and I am flustered beyond belief.

"FLOWERS." I jump as he shouts the word and Marcus looks away, already bored.

"Um, I don't know, really." Images of freshly picked blooms festooning every surface in this church call to the romantic in me and I wonder if Camilla can help me out with this by raiding her rose garden. Maybe I should be taking notes because so many things are whizzing around my mind as I contemplate a wedding in just a few days' time. I just shrug and mumble, "I think Mrs Hudson has that in hand already."

"BANS." I look at him in shock as I imagine we have somehow broken church rules and will be turned out on the street.

"Excuse me." He looks at Marcus and says loudly, "I have read them three times, and only your mother has witnessed it. I would have expected one of you in the congregation to hear them at least."

"We were, um, out of town." Marcus tries to think of a reason why we haven't done our duty, and I look at them in surprise. "They've been read already."

"Of course, this wedding has been in the planning even before you arrived. I thought you knew that."

"She did."

Marcus throws me a warning look and I nod miserably. "Of course, silly me, I forgot."

Harrison snaps his notebook shut with a resounding clap, and I jump as he stands and bellows. "See you tomorrow, 7 pm sharp. I will walk you through the procedures."

Without another word, he strides off to the back of the church and disappears through an archway, and I blink after him in shock.

Suddenly, silence replaces the conversation and the loud

bellowing of the slightly scary vicar, and I feel as if I've been in an emotional boxing ring. For some reason, I feel so weary, so beaten, and so false. Maybe I should kneel down and pray for my soul because it's doubtful mine is shining right now.

To my surprise, Marcus slips his hand in mine and squeezes it gently, and I look at him in surprise.

His eyes have that look in them which pulls me in and forgives him everything.

Leaning closer, his breath caresses my ear as he whispers, "Thank you. I know that was hard for you."

"It's fine." I bite my lip because once again I'm reminded this is just a favour, not real and I should stop thinking of it that way and then I'm surprised all over again as Marcus whispers, "I've got a surprise for you."

"What?"

I look around as if there is a surprise guest ready to jump out of the crevices of the church and he grins.

"I was thinking about our conversation earlier."

"Which one?" I try to think back to earlier, and he grins with a wicked look in his eye.

"You were right, you do deserve more, and I have taken for granted something I should have addressed the moment you said yes."

"What?" I am so confused right now, and he pulls me up and grins.

"You'll see."

As I follow him down the aisle, I wonder what he's playing at but, from the look in his eye, it's something I will hopefully like.

CHAPTER 20

I blink in surprise at the sight that greets me when we step outside the church. Brad is standing beside a huge camper van that gleams in the final rays of the departing sun.

"Your chariot awaits, babe."

Brad grins as Marcus sighs heavily beside me as we contemplate the home from home that is apparently revved up and ready to go.

"What's this?" I stare at it in shock and Brad grins.

"This is my pride and joy that Marcus talked me into lending you for a dirty night of passion."

He laughs out loud as I blush and Marcus growls, "Ignore him, Sammy. This is your dream; I wanted to make it come true."

Now I feel extremely awkward because this is more like my nightmare. When I pictured Marcus in a tent, it wasn't because I wanted to be in one. I was just imagining him out of his comfort zone and I'm not surprised he managed to find a loophole even in that by magically making a house on wheels appear instead.

To be honest, I've never been that kind of girl. One who camps and enjoys the rugged outdoors, but how can I tell him that now? He did this for me and despite the horror I'm feeling inside, I feel slightly touched by that.

Almost expecting him to turn around and hand me the keys, before heading back to Valley House for a night alone in his bed, I'm surprised when Brad tosses him the keys and says gruffly, "If there's one mark on her, I'll make you pay."

"As if." Marcus growls and Jake turns to me and smiles sweetly. "Enjoy your night among the stars, Sammy. It can get a little cold up at Pineland Forest, so make use of Marcus's body to keep warm, as a survival tactic, of course."

He laughs and then turns to walk away and I say in disbelief, "Where's he going, doesn't he need a lift home?"

Marcus shakes his head. "No, I'm guessing he's off to meet another one of his dates. She's probably waiting around the corner with the engine revving."

Watching his brother go reminds me of the local gossip and I wonder how many women's engines revved for him. Probably enough to stage a grand prix and I think back to his casual admission that he's already had sex. That was never in doubt, but I don't have to like it and so I say slightly huffily, "Don't we even get to go back and change."

Looking at my pink shift dress and stilettos, I wonder if this is such a good idea, and he says quickly, "No, Florrie packed some things for you and I hate to think what Jake packed for me. I called them earlier when you were at the Cosy Kettle picking up the afternoon coffee order."

"You did." For some reason, I'm touched by his actions because it's actually a really thoughtful thing to do. Mind you, I can just imagine Florrie laughing her head off at the thought of me camping – period.

She knows me so well and this is definitely not even on my bucket list, and I regret mentioning it all.

As Marcus holds open the door to our home for the night, I take a deep breath and suck it up because I asked for this in a weird roundabout way and he must never suspect for a second that I'm dreading every minute of it.

∼

BEING SO high up is empowering and I glance behind me at a home from home that is way more pleasant than I imagined.

"This is nice." I smile at Marcus as he starts the engine, and he sighs heavily, "If you say so."

Once again, he ruins a thoughtful deed with an attitude that rubs me up the wrong way and I turn and look out of the window, rather than make conversation with a man who is making it obvious he wishes he was anywhere else.

He flicks on the radio to Classic FM and a haunting melody fills the silence, leaving me to battle the wave of despair that is threatening to drag me under. Great, a whole night locked in this tin can on wheels with a man who has zero conversation and zero enthusiasm for being here.

As we eat up the miles, I stare at the scenery with interest because now we are heading in a different direction. The houses soon fade away, replaced by open countryside that is casting night shadows against the glare of our headlights.

I watch with interest, trying to ignore the fact I'm starving right now and Camilla's breakfast lecture is coming back to bite me. I couldn't even eat lunch because I was so wired up after Maria's claim on my man and I suppose that's when the doubts really began to creep in and take root.

"Where are we going?" I try to break the silence as we speed past trees and darkened hedges and Marcus sighs. "Pineland Forest. It's the best place to camp around here and Jake assured me he's stocked us with enough food to keep us going until tomorrow."

"I hope so." I am seriously hungry and say impulsively, "Isn't there a takeaway somewhere, or a nice cosy pub to eat in."

"No."

He turns the wheel and we head off up a dusty track and I see trees lining our route as the headlights pick out their shadows. A lone rabbit skips across the path in front of us and I quickly put my hand on Marcus's arm and gasp, "Watch out."

Luckily, the rabbit scampers off into the wilderness and Marcus chuckles as I sigh with relief.

"I take it rabbit stew's off the menu."

"It was never on it." I layer a hard edge to my voice because just the thought of eating Peter Rabbit is not a happy one.

"Is it far?"

Peering through the windscreen, all I can see is trees, and he nods. "A few minutes away. Hopefully there's no one else around. The last thing we need is neighbours."

"Why not?" I feel suddenly unsafe and say anxiously, "Surely there's safety in numbers, it would be better don't you think."

"Not really. This is the local dogging site and I'm not up for cameras being pointed in the window while I sleep."

"Dogging! Seriously."

He nods. "Just don't look if you see any cars parked, it will only encourage them."

"Turn this thing around – immediately."

I feel faint with anxiety and Marcus laughs out loud. "I'll protect you, angel. We have blinds at the window, anyway."

"But what if they, well, you know, loiter outside in the hope of an audio version at least?"

"Then they'll be disappointed, unless you have other ideas."

He laughs softly and I feel my cheeks on fire with embarrassment. "Of course not – no way. I was just… well, I was just putting myself in their position."

"I wouldn't do that, people will talk." He is openly laughing out loud now and I mentally have words with myself.

"This will do."

He pulls off the road into a clearing and I quickly look for other cars, vans or motorbikes and feel happy to see we're alone.

He cuts the engine and with it the music and suddenly it feels a very scary place to be.

Darkness is all around and the silence is deafening because now I have my turbulent thoughts to make me even crazier.

Marcus turns and crawls behind me. "Let's set up and get some food going. I think your bag is on the bed."

Scurrying after him, I see my holdall looking slightly strange next to Marcus's plain black one, probably because it has Sponge Bob Square Pants all over it.

He blinks in surprise at the quite ridiculous luggage choice and I say defensively, "Don't you dare diss Sponge Bob. I won't have it."

Laughing, he shakes his head and begins to remove his jacket and I say in alarm, "What are you doing?"

"Changing. I think there are some sweat pants in here and a hoodie. The sooner I make myself comfortable, the sooner we eat.

I quickly avert my eyes as he strips down to his boxers and I feel the heat building as I try to look anywhere but where I really want my eyes heading.

"You can look now." He grins as he stands before me, looking good enough to eat because casual Marcus is every bit as impressive as corporate Marcus.

"Your turn." He smirks and I say crossly, "Some privacy please."

Shrugging, he turns his back on me and I rifle through the bag like a desperate woman at the biggest sale in town.

My heart sinks when I see the Victoria Secrets joggers that Florrie must have packed with 'sexy' written across the back of it. The matching hoody has white fur trimmed around the hood with 'sexy babe' emblazoned on the back. The slightly revealing satin vest top is sending all the wrong signals and mentally I kill Florrie a million times. There isn't even anything else to disguise it with, so I say through gritted teeth. "Ok, you can turn around now, but don't laugh. Florrie obviously has a seriously twisted sense of humour and in my defence, I bought this for a knockdown price in the sale."

He spins around and I feel that infernal heat spreading through me again as his eyes glitter as he rakes me in from head to toe. It feels like a sexual act as he shifts slightly closer and touches the fur on the hoodie with a look in his eyes that tells me every thought in his head right now.

"I like it."

He is almost salivating, and I bat his hand away and say roughly, "I bet you do. Anyway, I'm starving. What did they pack?"

He turns to the mini kitchen area and I peer over his shoulder at the fridge door and as he opens it, I see some steak wrapped in brown paper and a couple of jacket potatoes.

"Not bad." Marcus smiles with relief as he pulls out a bottle of wine that is resting on the shelf inside the fridge door.

"I'll start up the barbeque and you can pour the drinks. It won't take long if we throw the potatoes in the fire and cook the steaks.

He heads outside and luckily, the cool breeze enters the

van and calms my heated libido. Fortunately, I'm alone right now and can watch him undetected as he struggles with the matches needed to light the disposable barbeque.

Despite the shock of being here, dressed like a Victoria Secrets model, I am looking forward to a night under the stars. Glancing across at the rather small bed, I wonder how that will work. Marcus's bed at Valley House is absolutely huge and we could exist there without ever touching but this is a completely different story and by the looks of it, we will have to top and tail because the alternative is making me feel weak at the knees.

Wandering outside, I hand him a glass of wine and he says with his usual authority, "There should be a couple of fold up chairs in there somewhere. Grab a blanket too, it's turning a bit cooler and you don't want to catch a chill."

Quickly, I do as he says and locate them under the bed and soon, we have quite a cosy camp set up, made even cosier by the glowing candles I found in the cupboard. Thinking of who owns this van, I wonder how many times he's parked it at this dogging site and a small giggle escapes me, making Marcus say with interest, "What's so funny?"

"It's just, well, I was picturing Brad bringing his dates up here and mixing with the doggers."

"He does. In fact, he should have a reserved space; the man's out of control."

"What do you think he'll do about the inheritance?"

When we were cruising, Marcus told me that there were five parts to his father's will. His mother got the lodge house and enough money to keep her accustomed to her lifestyle and the rest was divided into four parts. Marcus wants the house and land, which goes to the first son who marries. The second son gets the building business, and the third gets the money in the bank and savings. The fourth and final inheritance is the stocks and shares and I know that Jake has his sights set on that one, which is why he's in the best position possible, because he can wait for the others to make their moves and claim the rest.

Florrie is in no hurry to marry, due to the fact she was on honeymoon when she met Jake, with me as her companion after her groom turned out to be married to someone else at the time. Marcus and Dom are the only two who want the same thing, which is why they saw me coming and recognised a pushover when they saw one.

In answer to my question, Marcus shrugs. "He'll wait for the money because he would hate the business and the house, for that matter. He never wanted responsibility and just wants to travel, so the money will help with that."

"And you just want to develop a small kingdom, and Dom wants to keep things just as they are. Do you think he'll rustle up a wedding certificate before we sign ours? I wouldn't put it past him."

"No."

Marcus is obviously sure about that and I say with curiosity, "Why are you so sure?"

"Because of mum. She would be destroyed if he married behind her back and even his dreams aren't worth tearing her heart out."

His words remind me I'm doing just that and I fight the tears as I think about my own parents, my brother even, as they find out what I've done. If things go according to Marcus's plan, it's doubtful they ever will, but what if?

Almost as if he's a mind reader, Marcus says softly, "Have you told your parents yet?"

"No." I turn away and bite my lip to stop the tears from falling and once again, he surprises me by crouching down before me and saying apologetically, "I'm sorry, angel. You must feel so alone."

It's too much and as he pulls me against him and strokes my hair, the tears fall because I wish this was different so badly. I wish it was a real wedding, where my parents sat watching with pride in their eyes, not this - contract.

"Tell them, Sammy, invite them." He sounds so sincere, and it breaks my heart.

"No." I push him away and take a few deep breaths.

"No." I say it again, a little louder because I will not make them watch me make a fool of myself.

"Why not?" He sounds confused and I say shortly, "Because it's not real. Because you are paying me to marry you and because…"

I look down and whisper, "Because you don't love me."

A nearby owl hoots in the distance, and the fire crackles as the scent of char-grilled meat fills the air. Cursing, Marcus breaks the spell and says quickly, "Grab a couple of plates, angel, the food's burning."

Glad of the distraction, I head inside and emerge a few seconds later with a couple of plates and some cutlery.

As Marcus dishes up, I have a strict word with my heart and when he hands me the plate with concern in his eyes, I smile shakily. "Thanks, this looks good enough to eat."

His slightly worried smile makes me look away as I sit on the fold up chair with the blanket wrapped around me.

He follows my lead and we are soon eating what is turning out to be a very impressive meal.

"Does food always taste better like this?"

I speak through my mouthful of meat and he laughs. "I've always thought so."

As we eat under the stars, despite the cool wind fanning the flames, I feel a happiness I wasn't expecting. Somehow, out here, normal life is placed on hold. It's as if we are on our own planet and I laugh softly.

"What's so funny?"

"Nothing."

He raises his eyes and I laugh. "I was just thinking it's as if we're on our own planet."

"Sounds good. What shall we call it?"

"Samus."

He grins. "Mammy."

"Rubbish."

"Ok, Samus it is. So, what do the inhabitants of Samus do?"

"They chill."

I shiver in the wind's arms and he laughs out loud. "You've got that right."

Standing up, he takes my empty plate and heads into the van before emerging with what looks like a hip flask.

"Here, medicinal brandy, to take the chill away."

I take a grateful swig and cough frantically as the bite of the alcohol catches me unaware.

Handing it back to him, he takes a swig of his own with an accompanying wink and drags his chair beside mine, nearer the fire. I'm surprised when he places his arm around my shoulders and pulls me closer, whispering, "Shared body heat, it's called saving your life."

"Maybe I'm saving yours."

Suddenly, he looks more serious and stares into my eyes, making me hold my breath, as he whispers, "You already have."

For some reason, we have created a moment in time that changes everything. He looks so vulnerable out here, as if his heart is exposed and I can't look away. It appears that neither can he and like a magnetic pull, our lips hover dangerously close and as they come together, a thousand fireworks explode in my head as Marcus kisses me for real for the first time since we met.

There is no one around, nobody to impress or to fool into thinking we're a couple. This is because he wants it. I want this, I always have and as we kiss like any normal couple, the relief settles any doubts I ever had.

CHAPTER 21

A loud bang wakes me and I struggle to remember where I am.

"Open up!"

For some reason, I appear to be tangled up in someone's legs and as we bump heads when we try to jump up, it all comes rushing back.

After sharing a delicious kiss, Marcus took me to bed - to keep warm. We just snuggled down and shared body heat while we talked and kissed some more, just like any other couple. It was strictly kissing only and now it appears we are being raided.

"Do you think it's the doggers?"

I stare at Marcus with wide eyes and he growls, "Unlikely, but wait here, I'll see what's happening."

Pulling him back, I hiss, "Don't go out there. It could be anyone. Probably a biker gang, or mafia. They may attack you and leave you for dead before abducting me into slavery."

I feel genuinely afraid, but it appears Marcus is anything but as he says angrily, "I hope whoever it is can run fast."

"Open up, this is the police. We've got you surrounded."

"Oh, my god." My hand flies to my mouth and my eyes are wide as I look at Marcus in horror. "The police!" I hiss the word and he rolls his eyes. "This is all I need."

Throwing the door open, he shields his eyes as a flashlight shines in his face and I hear, "Is that you, Marcus?"

"Yes, who is it?"

It appears that whoever it is has blinded Marcus and I hear a soft chuckle. "You had better come out; we're rounding them up."

Them?

Marcus sighs as the officer says casually, "Are you alone in there, mate?"

"I'm with my fiancée. What's this all about, Bob?"

I flick a nervous look at my holdall and swear Sponge Bob winks at me.

"You'd better call her and step outside, sorry and all but rules are rules."

Marcus sighs and holds out his hand. "Come on, angel, let's get this over with."

Wrapping the blanket around me, I follow him outside and stare around in shock.

Marcus growls, "What the hell?"

As I look, the area is swamped with cars and vans. A small crowd of people are standing shivering in the cold night air in varying stages of undress. There is a police car with its blue lights flashing and lots of complaints turning the air as blue as the sirens.

"What's happening?" I inch closer to Marcus and am grateful when he tucks me into his side wrapping a strong, protective arm around me and sighs. "It appears our campsite has attracted a lot more visitors."

The police officer stands before us and I shrink under his knowing look as he holds a pencil to his pocketbook.

"Sorry guys, I need your name for the records."

"For what reason, we've done nothing wrong?"

Marcus sounds angry and I don't blame him and listen with dismay as the officer leans forward and whispers, "We've been told to clean up Pineland Forest. These doggers are getting out of hand and the local MP wants it shut down. We're taking down everyone's particulars and issuing them with a warning."

"We're just camping for goodness's sake." Marcus sounds so frustrated and I am now extremely worried about the impending criminal record I could get for sex crimes.

"That's what they all say."

Marcus looks as if he's about to lose any cool he has left and I step in and smile. "The thing is, officer, we *are* camping. We actually have a camper van and the remnants of a barbeque to prove it. When we got here, the place was deserted and we never even knew the other cars arrived. Please, you must believe us."

Bob, the police officer, looks around and leans closer, whispering, "Leave it with me. I'll write your names with invisible ink; it will be our secret."

"Marcus, babe, I thought that was you."

I jump as a loud shriek floats across the wooded area and Marcus groans. "Great, that's all I need."

Officer Bob looks suspicious as a woman looking extremely worse for wear cries out, "You never called me. Did you lose my number or something?"

By now, everyone's attention is firmly on us and if we were hoping to go unnoticed, it was a false hope because I think someone is even videoing us on their phone.

"No, I just didn't call."

Marcus doesn't even try to pretend, and she looks at him angrily. "That's a bit rude, isn't it?"

Marcus has obviously had enough because he finally

snaps and says to officer Bob. "Listen, we've done nothing wrong and certainly aren't here for the reason you think. If you think differently, you can take it up with my solicitor. Now, if you'll excuse us, we were having a nice evening before we were so rudely interrupted."

He turns and I worry about that because you should never turn your back on a police officer. I mean, he may think you're resisting arrest and taser you or something, so I pull him back and say politely, "I'm sorry, officer Bob, but Marcus is right. Please, we've done nothing wrong and well, it's my wedding in two days' time, and we could really do without the scandal right now. Please make sure to stop by and celebrate with us, but Marcus is right, we've done nothing wrong."

"Ok, you can go."

Bob snaps his notebook shut and sighs. "To be honest, I tried to get out of this one. Two days ago, they would have caught me in the act, so who I am to judge? No, you're lucky it was me, mate, and not Sergeant Driscoll. He would arrest the lot of you on sight and ask questions later."

He turns to look at the disgruntled people who are complaining about police harassment, and Marcus sighs. "Thanks, Bob. I'll catch up with you later."

He almost drags me inside the camper van and slams the door before saying gruffly, "I need a drink."

Removing the brandy from the side, he unscrews the cap before handing it to me and I take a long sip, just grateful for the warmth it gives me.

"Who was that woman?" Despite everything that just happened, I can only think of her and Marcus sighs.

"Donna, the barmaid from the Blue Balls."

"The what?"

I can't help but giggle and he grins. "Mad, isn't it, anyway she's a terrible flirt and is always dishing out her number to the customers as if she's advertising for a date and as always it goes straight in the bin. I'm not surprised to see her up here. I would have put money on it."

"Really, The Blue Balls, wow."

Giggling, I take another sip of the brandy as we hear more shouting outside and I collapse back on the bed and crawl inside, just desperate to feel some warmth. Propping myself up, I hold on tight to the flask and Marcus smiles sweetly. "Shall I make us a hot drink? I think Brad has a camping stove somewhere in here."

"That would be great."

As he starts rifling through cupboards and drawers, I watch him work and for once feel happier about our situation. He has surprised me tonight. From the camping trip to the barbeque and then that kiss. Afterwards, we talked until we fell asleep and I thought nothing about being wrapped in his arms. Now this. I kind of like this side of him. The one where he lets his guard down a little and shows he's human after all. I wonder if he's just reacting to the conversation we had earlier when I expressed my doubts. It could be an act but that kiss, it felt so right, so normal, and it changed everything.

CHAPTER 22

When we finally wake up, we are wrapped in one another as if our bodies decided it was a necessary precaution for survival. We are still wearing our lounge wear and, for a moment, I lie still and enjoy the unexpected turn of events. Last night was magical for a host of different reasons. Marcus opened up a little and dropped his usual guard and I liked it. The fact we were nearly arrested for sex crimes was a minor inconvenience, funny even, but doesn't dampen my spirits and I wonder what will happen now.

Ever since I met Marcus on the cruise, I have longed for a closer relationship with him. When he asked me to marry him for financial gain, I didn't hesitate, which shocks me. I'm not the sort of person who does things for money, but I would do anything for love. Now I know what Meatloaf was talking about when he sang that particular song because apparently love blinds you to common sense and turns you slightly mad. Well, if this is madness, I'm a happy woman because every dream I ever had is coming true as I lie wrapped in the limbs of the man I'm to marry and wonder if just possibly, there may be a tiny ray of hope this may all work out in the end.

"Remind me never to go camping again."

Marcus's husky voice makes me smile as his hold tightens on me, which makes my heart sing. Rather than jump up with a whole load of regrets, he seems quite happy with the situation and I say with smug contentment, "Well, I enjoyed it, even the misunderstanding."

"Then you're a strange woman, Sammy Jo, who gets her kicks in the weirdest of ways."

His low rumble of laughter makes me smile, and I could even imagine waking up in his arms every day for the rest of my life.

"Brad has a lot to answer for."

"Why?" I'm surprised because Brad has done us a huge favour, in my mind anyway.

"Telling me to come here, despite its reputation. We could have camped at the Dream Valley caravan park by Rocky Cove and had none of this madness."

"I kind of like a little madness in my life."

He shifts onto his side and it feels a little disconcerting as he stares into my eyes and I immediately stress out about the way I look. I'm guessing it's not a pleasant sight and yet he is smiling and once again lets my hair filter through his fingers as if he's fascinated by it.

"You're so pretty, Sammy."

His unexpected compliment takes me by surprise and I'm not sure what to say. Do I compliment him back, or just giggle like a love sick fool? I'm guessing hair tie woman would purr seductively and inch a little closer, raking her gel-polished fingernail down his cheek and whispering, 'Then feel free to mess me up a little,' or something sexy like that.

Instead, I just blush as always and deny everything. "No,

I'm not pretty. Goodness, you must still be dreaming. I mean, look at me, I must look as if I've been dragged through a hedge on repeat." Pinching him, I giggle at the horror on his face as I giggle, "You must still be dreaming, let me wake you up."

He grins and says in his husky drawl, "You're right, I must have been dreaming. Have you seen yourself this morning?"

Laughing, I roll over and stare up at the ceiling and say, "So, what now? Is it straight to work in yesterday's clothes, or do we head back and enjoy a Mrs Jenkins special?"

"We head home."

He shifts down the bed and jumps out, and the disappointment I feel about that shocks me. I'm not ready for this magical night to end and return to what it was yesterday. For one moment there, I felt as if we were a normal couple, not a business arrangement.

I watch as he busies himself tidying things away, and he says over his shoulder, "No need to change or anything, we can do that at home."

Home. One word that wraps my heart in rainbows and makes me think I really do belong here. It may have only been a couple of days and I wonder if home could change in a heartbeat when Marcus gets his way, because he will. I'm in no doubt about that and sitting up, I hug my knees to my chest and say with interest, "What happens to everyone when you start the development?"

"Nothing."

"Will it affect Valley House, your family?"

"Not really. I have ring-fenced a large area of land around it so despite what my brothers think, nothing will change for us except we capitalise on our assets and ensure our future."

"Will you continue to live with them? What happens if they marry, where will they go?"

"That's up to them. I'm guessing their own inheritance

will give them the capital to build their own houses if they want to. I know Brad would be content to live in this camper van. Jake will probably move to Riverton because he likes a busier town and Dom, well, he will probably stay put just to irritate me and remind me of everything I've done wrong in life on a daily basis."

"And your mother?"

He smiles and I love how much he loves her. "She will be moving into the lodge house. It's all arranged. We're renovating it to her specifications and she can still use Valley House as her home if she likes. Mum's future is guaranteed with me, or any of us really."

"What if she marries again? It could happen, you know. How would you feel about another man in your midst?"

He sits on the edge of the bed and looks at me thoughtfully. "You have a lot of questions for an early start. I'm exhausted already." He grins and I nudge him gently.

"I'm just curious. There's nothing wrong with a little dose of curiosity to feed an enquiring mind, you know."

Shaking his head, his low rumble of laughter makes me smile, and then he reaches for my hand and laces his fingers with mine.

"This is nice."

"It is."

We share yet another smile and he seems about to say something else, but then checks himself before looking at his watch.

"We should go, we have a busy day."

My heart sinks as the magic is broken and I sigh. "Yes, I suppose we have."

I make to move but he hangs onto my hand and says quickly, "We won't be working today though, there's no time for that."

"Really?" I look up in surprise and he groans.

"Sorry, angel, but you have a full day with my mother and Florrie. You need to transform into the perfect bride and don't have long. The wedding is tomorrow and I'm sorry about that but well, you know."

"I know." Taking a deep sigh, I am brought right back to the reason I'm here at all and my heart sinks as business takes over once again.

"What will you do?"

"Make myself into the perfect bridegroom, of course."

He winks and despite the nature of our union, I still feel excited about it because one thing is certain, I'm marrying the man of my dreams tomorrow and I have two years to make it real.

CHAPTER 23

The smirks on just about everyone's faces at breakfast make my heart race a little as we walk hand in hand into the dining room at Valley House a short while later.

The fact one face looks like thunder makes my heart sink, reminding me that not everyone is happy about this.

It's a full house this morning and Brad and Dom are sitting beside Camilla and Florrie and I do everything I can not to look into the madness of Dom's eyes.

"Sammy, darling, I can only apologise for my son's lack of judgement in making you sleep in the wild last night. You poor thing, you must have had a terrible ordeal." Camilla sounds upset for me and I catch Florrie's eye, who is trying not to laugh and my lips twitch as I say brightly. "It was lovely, very thoughtful actually."

Brad starts to laugh and says cheekily, "It's all over the local Facebook page that Pineland Forest was raided last night. In fact, there's even a video placing you both at the scene."

"What?" I stare at him in horror as Marcus groans.

"I blame you for this, Brad. We both know it should be you named and shamed, not me."

"Show me." Camilla sounds strangely excited, and it makes me smile as Brad hands her his phone and she laughs gleefully. "Marcus, you look so angry, and who are those people nearby? Did they forget their clothes or something? My oh my, I should get up there and check this out for myself."

"Your battery is flat; you'd never make it." Dom sounds angry and she shrugs. "I'll charge it up then. Can I borrow your outfit, Sammy? I love the fur detail, so pretty."

Just picturing Camilla wearing my 'sexy angel' outfit makes me laugh and Florrie grins as I roll my eyes in her direction, blaming her entirely for my outfit choice.

"We should do that sometimes, babe." Jake is stroking her hair and once again I feel a pang as I see the love in his eyes and she smiles as if they are sharing a delicious secret. "Sounds like fun."

We take our seats as Mrs Jenkins appears, and by the time we place our order, the conversation has turned to another subject and Marcus whispers, "I'll get that video taken down, don't worry, angel, leave it with me."

He grabs some toast and starts smearing it with marmalade, and I think about the man I'm marrying. He's so practical, caring even in a strange way, but emotionally he's not really there yet. I wonder why he doesn't have a girlfriend because a man like him could pick and choose, but for some reason he's alone and I wonder if we're more similar than I first thought. Like me, he probably just never met the right one and it would be interesting to know what he's thinking about our own situation.

I can feel Dom's eyes on me and refuse to look because I doubt I'd like what I see in them. He knows the real story here and I wonder if he disapproves because he wanted to use me in the same way. Then again, maybe he really did have feelings for me that I knocked back so cruelly.

"Girls, we have such a fun day planned."

Camilla's excited voice breaks through my thoughts and she smiles. "After breakfast, we're heading to Riverton to buy our dresses. Such an exciting moment and then we will lunch and after that have mani-pedis and a glass of champagne to celebrate. Then we will return home for an early night before the fun begins."

She turns to Marcus. "Make yourself scare, darling. Maybe you should sleep in the guest room tonight, or better still in a hotel because we don't want to break the tradition where the groom can't see his bride before their wedding day."

"It's fine." I look at him in surprise as he says quickly, "I have places to go and may not be back until the early hours, anyway."

"Where?" Camilla voices the word screaming in my head right now as I sense Marcus may be making the most of his last night of freedom, which makes me insanely jealous and brings out my possessive claws. Wondering if Maria is on the menu again, I feel sick as I push my fruit around the yoghurt smeared bowl and try not to look miserable.

"Just business – as always."

Maybe it's just my heightened emotions playing tricks on me, but it feels like Marcus is hiding something because he quickly changes the subject and says to his brothers collectively, "The suits are ready for collection. Jake, can I rely on you to collect them? I think that's all I needed to do."

"Are you sure, darling, what about the stag do? Surely you need to spend the evening tied to a flagpole naked or something."

Camilla laughs, and Marcus shakes his head. "No need for that. I'm not one for tradition, anyway."

Once again, I feel the man I discovered last night slipping from my fingers as he reverts back to the cold-hearted one he really is, reminding me this isn't a real wedding and why should he bother with everything that usually goes with that. He can't even be bothered to pick up his own suit and I feel suddenly weary with it all.

Florrie is looking concerned and I can't deal with that right now either and just wish tomorrow was over already because then at least I can start my new life in Dream Valley under the radar. They will soon lose interest and I can relax knowing the hardest decision of my life so far has been made, and I have kept my side of the bargain.

∼

AFTER BREAKFAST, Marcus disappears, leaving me waiting for Camilla with a worried best friend. As we wait in the living room, Florrie lowers her voice and says with concern, "There's still time to change your mind, you really don't have to do this."

"I know."

There's an awkward silence and then she sighs. "Why are you really doing this, Sammy? I know you and this isn't like you. You always wanted the fairy tale, and this really isn't it. Do you think it will change; are you hoping for more because if you are, you should apply the brakes and make Marcus work hard for your heart?"

"I do want this, Florrie, you're right. I'm not that cold, you know. I'm doing this because I want to marry him. Don't ask me why, he hasn't really given me any reason to think it's anything other than a means to an end, but I want what you have with Jake and I'm prepared to put a little work into that."

"Oh, Sammy." Florrie looks upset for me and I bite my lip

as Camilla floats into the room in a chiffon dress, with her hair tied in a messy bun on top of her head.

"We should get going, darlings, our appointment is soon and I can't wait to sit and watch a fashion show of the best kind. It will be just like, 'Say Yes To The Dress' and just so you know, this is my treat and I'm happy to say yes to whichever one you like."

I feel even worse now when I see the happiness in her eyes and Florrie looks worried because the purchase of these dresses can resemble a small mortgage.

"I couldn't..." I try to protest, but she fixes me with a hard look and says firmly, "I insist. I don't have a daughter to spoil, and now I have two. Please don't rain on my parade, I've been dreaming of this day forever it seems."

The tears aren't that far away when I think of who should be excited about today. I never imagined for one moment that my own mother wouldn't be there at my wedding dress fitting and I'm feeling the effects of my decision not to include her. What if this is it and Marcus does fall in love with me? She will never have that experience. I will be married already and I'm denying her something she has probably imagined a thousand times since I was born.

It's too much and I hesitate as Camilla says brightly, "Come on, darlings, let's hope Brad charged the car and we're not stranded again."

"We could take mine." Florrie breathes a sigh of relief and even Camilla looks happy about that as she nods. "Good idea. Well, what are we waiting for?"

As we head off, I pull my heavy heart behind me because this is already proving to be a very emotional, difficult day, and tomorrow's not looking good either.

CHAPTER 24

*H*appy Endings is an upmarket bridal shop on a smart street in a bustling town. Riverton, unlike Dream Valley, has many shops and cafes and a thriving community. It took us just over thirty minutes to get here and I like what I see. Camilla directs me to the public car park and we are soon standing outside a shop that makes my heart beat a little faster as I contemplate the choice I'm about to make.

"Mrs Hudson." The elegant woman inside greets us as soon as we step through the door and I look around at a fairy tale. Rows of gorgeous dresses hang with pride in a pretty, elegant interior, with a huge chandelier hanging from the centre.

Florrie nudges me and says with concern, "Are you ok, Sammy?"

Fixing a bright smile on my face, I nod. "Never better."

Florrie's expression tells me she doesn't believe a word of it and I'm glad for Camilla's excitement as she takes up residence on the chaise longue and pats the space beside her.

"Come and sit beside me, Florence. Mrs Everhard will

help Sammy Jo decide on a few dresses."

Resisting the urge to giggle at Florrie's expression as she stares at Mrs Everhard with a smile on her face, I follow the beaming lady along the rows of dresses.

Just looking at these creations makes my heart beat a little faster because they are the stuff of fairy tales. Frills, lace and finery crowd my mind and make me feel like a princess.

I'm not sure what I prefer, a full-length meringue style dress, or a smooth, sophisticated gown that hugs my curves and makes me feel sexy and regal at the same time.

Deciding to try a few different styles, I make my selection and head into the changing room where Mrs Everhard hangs a white silk robe.

"Change into this, my dear, but keep on your underwear. The cubicles are too small to accommodate some of the dresses and so I will help you into them out here."

The floor-length mirror reflects my excitement because despite everything, I have always dreamed of this moment and am caught up in the occasion.

Making short work of changing, I am soon dressed in the silk robe and Mrs Everhard says quickly, "Which one first?"

My eye is drawn to a rather full dress with a massive train and I say with a whisper, "That one."

I watch as she heaves the monstrous creation off the hanger and I prepare myself to be dressed like Cinderella by her fairy godmother.

By the time she finishes I have run through every dream I ever had as I finally live out the moment I think I've been preparing for ever since I heard Cinderella's story.

However, as I look at my reflection in the oversized mirror, I feel – nothing.

Searching harder, deeper, for that spark that surely should accompany this dress, I find absolutely nothing and with a pang I realise it's because *she's* not here – my mum.

Just the thought of heading out to show the others doesn't feel right somehow. They aren't the ones I want to see me in my wedding dress for the very first time. It should be the woman who has always been there for me and now she's not. Because I didn't trust her with the single most important detail of my life – I'm getting married.

Mrs Everhard looks at me with appreciation and says brightly, "You look beautiful, my dear. Such a picture. I bet you can't wait for your family to see you in that dress."

Her words cause a reaction neither of us was expecting as I burst into tears and bury my face in my hands and sob, "I can't do this."

It's too much. I want my mum and I want to stamp my foot like a toddler and make her come running. This isn't right, so wrong on every level and all because I was protecting her from discovering her daughter is an idiot and can't be trusted to make an adult decision.

I feel like I'm hiding something I've done wrong, like when I wet my Tuesday knickers and buried them in the garden. For some time, Tuesday was missing from my life. Or the time I broke her favourite figurine, the one she had saved up for with her pin money, as she called it, and I was so worried I blamed the cat. But it was me – always me because I could never own up to anything and still can't.

Mrs Everhard pats my back and whispers words of encouragement like 'It's natural.' 'Brides are always so emotional' and 'I can recommend drugs for this.'

But the only thing I need is my mum and if I'm a mess now, what on earth will I be like tomorrow when I have to walk down that aisle without my dad?

A fresh burst of tears escapes at that thought and now Mrs Everhard is getting alarmed as she sprints off murmuring, "Alcohol is the answer on this occasion," and I feel bad for her. I feel bad for myself and I feel bad for my family. And for Camilla and Florence, who are the only ones excited in all of this.

Staring at my tear-streaked face, I wonder for the millionth time if I'm doing the right thing and then from out of nowhere comes a gentle buzzing from the cubicle.

Sniffing, I grab the phone and see a message came through from Marcus, and my heart skips a beat when I see his name on the screen. I'm doing this because of him. The complicated man who intrigues me. He did from the very first time I met him, and I don't know why. He's an enigma, rather distant and a little cool sometimes, but that act has me hooked. Then there's the softer side of him I'm discovering I like even more and yet it's all an act – on his part, anyway.

Clicking on the message, I see three words that confuse me.

Because I do.

Is he drunk? What does this even mean? Is he referring to his marriage vows, which reminds me I still haven't written mine? Maybe there's one on google I can copy and insert our names in it. Whatever I come up with will be way more emotional than the contract he's probably drawing up at his solicitors as we speak. He said he had a busy day after all and yet, what does this mean?

Mrs Everhard runs back with a glass filled with what could be Vodka. Looking so concerned I feel bad all over again and as she thrusts it in my hand, the shop doorbell rings and she sighs. "Goodness, it's all happening. Maybe I should advertise for staff. This is going to be one of those days."

As she leaves in a fluster, I stare back at my reflection and sigh.

I can do this. I've made my bed, and it's time to lie in it. Every cliché rolls around my mind as I give myself a very stern talking to and so, with a deep breath and a wish I had pinched the hip flask from the camper van, I head out to see what the others think.

As I try to negotiate the dress through the door, I'm a little distracted at first and then, as I look up with a little irritation, I blink as if Mrs Everhard somehow slipped me those drugs she recommended because I think I'm hallucinating.

Standing watching me, with tears in her eyes and an expression of complete and utter devotion, is my mother.

I blink furiously and look again, but she's still there and says softly, "You look beautiful, Sammy Jo."

"Mum."

I whisper the word as if I'm dreaming, and she nods. "You didn't think I'd miss my own daughter's wedding, did you?"

I look at Florrie who is openly sobbing as Camilla pats her back and offers her a hanky from her travel pack and I wonder if Florence told on me.

Feeling as if I've been caught out, I shift nervously on my satin heels and say shakily, "How did you know?"

"A mother always knows, darling, it's called the maternal instinct."

"Wow." I am so impressed right now because who knew that was a real thing.

Camilla smiles through her misty expression.

"You look like an angel."

Her words cause my heart to flutter because just that word reminds me of the man I'm marrying and there it is again, that burst of excitement, that feeling of finding the prince that makes your soul shiver and your heart to race.

Because I do.

I am still struggling with that and then mum steps forward and somehow manages to find me among this dress and hugs me so hard I can't breathe for a very different reason this time.

"I love you, sweetie, and you have made me so proud."

"I'm not so sure about that, mum."

She steps back and fixes me with that fierce look she always wore so well whenever I needed her to step up and take charge. The one where she would fight like a bear protecting its cub and slay an army just because they upset me in some way.

"Now dry your tears and let's get this party started. We can talk later but know this first. I am proud of you and I always have been, and this is no exception. So, what do you think of this dress? Is this the one?"

She looks at Florrie and Camilla and smiles. "What do you think?"

Florrie smiles, "I like it but there's something I don't like about the top."

"I know what you mean, darling, it's not very flattering, a little too low in my opinion and she could well, um, slip out at the most inopportune moment."

Looking down in horror, I realise I am revealing a little too much cleavage, way too much, and Mrs Everhard shakes her head. "We may need some magic tape for that, there's not enough support."

As they stare at my breasts, I feel extremely flustered and mum says with a laugh, "Typical Sammy Jo. She was always exposing herself unnecessarily on the beach when the string bikini shifted and earned her a reputation as a flasher. It didn't help that there was a school trip, and she was told off for exposing herself to children. Oh, how we laughed."

"Mum!" I stare at her in horror as she wipes the tears from her eyes. "Maybe you should try a different one because it's doubtful they do a strong enough tape for those beasts."

Florrie starts laughing and Camilla shakes her head and at least she's trying not to laugh at my humiliation, but I don't care. I could stand naked in the shop window for all I care because my mum's here and that's all that matters.

CHAPTER 25

I never knew there were so many types of wedding dresses. This is serious business and I think I make way through Mrs Everhard's entire stock. I have worn sexy slinky ones, full-blown meringues and even a few coloured ones. Nets underneath and those with huge trains that trip me up and yet I keep on going back to one in particular. Not as huge as some but understated elegance with silk and an embroidered bodice. A long flowing train that swishes as I walk and the veil Mrs Everhard recommends is the most beautiful thing I have ever seen.

Imagining myself sweeping up the aisle to meet the man who has corrupted my mind already makes me excited for the unknown. The sheer disaster that could end up happening just because I want to marry him so badly. Who cares if he's not fussed? He will be; maybe it will strike him like a thunderbolt when he turns and sees me looking like an angel. His angel, walking towards him with purpose and resolve. He could fall completely in love with me and reveal he always was. Miracles can happen and why not on the single most important day of a woman's life - before children, of course.

Wow, imagine that. Imagine we really make it that far. Just thinking of what that involves makes me feel weak at the knees and mum hands me a glass of champagne and says firmly, "So, darling, is this the one?"

As I spin around and look at my reflection in the huge mirror behind me, I feel so emotional I can only nod.

"Yes." My voice catches in my throat as I stare at the one. A dress that has been imagined a thousand times. Eagerly anticipated and dreamed about in my own personal fairy tale. I can't believe I'm meeting it at last. The reflection staring back at me is the one I always hoped to see. Like a welcome friend who made it despite the odds. The woman I always wanted to be but never thought would arrive. Now she's here, it's a little anticlimactic because the woman staring back at me is a fraud. She shouldn't be here because it's not her time.

Three voices ring out "So, are you saying..."

I stare at the imposter and take a deep breath because I've always been an impulsive fool and nothing will ever change that, so I mentally shrug and push the doubts away, giving into the moment and making it mine.

Smiling, I turn and say, "I'm saying yes to the dress."

Claps and cheers fill the small shop and Mrs Everhard is cheering the loudest because this dress, for all its understated glory, is carrying a hefty price tag. Apparently, it's been woven from silkworms in a fairy-strewn meadow if you believe Mrs Everhard's explanation of the reason for that and I wipe my tears away as this wedding suddenly becomes a lot more real.

Camilla looks so happy it heaps a whole lot of guilt on me as I think about the reason for this wedding at all. She thinks we're in love. At least one of us is, so that surely counts for something.

Because I do.

Suddenly, it hits me and it's like a knockout punch as the words echo around my mind and I push them away quickly, thinking I'm just clutching at rainbows.

Turning to my mum, I say quickly, "How did you know about this?"

She smiles and looks at Camilla, who is looking a little confused right now and says happily, "Marcus told us."

"Marcus did."

She nods. "He called yesterday and filled us in. I must say Sammy Jo, I was shocked. We both were because you've pulled off some stunts in your time but marriage, so soon. I felt as if I was in an episode of Married at First Sight."

I swallow hard as I feel like I'm going to be grounded or something and she whispers, "Marcus explained everything and we are so proud of you, darling. He's a very lucky man and let me say when he picked us up at the train station and brought us here, I realised you are a very lucky woman. He's utterly gorgeous."

"Marcus brought you here. Is he outside? Where's dad?"

I feel frantic right now and peer through the window, just hoping he hasn't been watching me all this time, especially during the exposing incident. I feel quite heated at that possibility.

"He's taken your father off for a suit and a chat, man to man."

"Oh." I catch Florrie's eye and she smiles her encouragement and I down the rest of my champagne in one go.

"Mrs Everhard is reaching for one herself, in celebration of the profit she's made today which reminds me Camilla is reaching into her purse and waving her credit card and I say quickly, "Please, I can't let you pay for this, it's too much."

Mum nods in agreement and says firmly, "I will pay."

"No mum, it's too much, maybe I should…"

"Samantha Josephine Hermione Miles. I cringe as the rest of the room looks up in stunned disbelief.

"I will be paying for your wedding dress and that's an end to it. I have been saving for this moment since the day I saw that pregnancy test turn positive and you will not deny your own mother her right."

Camilla nods as if she understands what she's saying, and I wonder if it's that maternal instinct again. Praying I have the magic in me somewhere too if I ever have that pleasure, I look at Florrie with a helplessness that causes her to grin.

"It's ok, babe." She nods her approval and I laugh nervously. "Ok."

Seeing Florrie sitting there looking slightly flushed by the fact she's been drinking all morning, I blurt out,

"We need a bridesmaid's dress for Florrie."

Mrs Everhard almost cheers as she grabs Florrie's hand and says quickly, "Come with me, my dear, I have the perfect dress in mind."

Looking slightly shocked, Florrie is pulled around the shop as Mrs Everhard piles dresses into her arms and they disappear into the cubicle, leaving mum to help me out of my own choice.

Camilla opens another bottle of champagne and says happily, "This is a very pleasant way to spend the day. I may well make it a weekly visit. Thank God I have four sons and who knows, I may even get married again myself. Then everyone can renew their vows, possibly annually. Yes, I think that could work. It would be worth it just for this alone."

Shaking my head, I head back to the changing room and hear Florrie inside her own cubicle with an excited Mrs Everhard.

As mum unzips the dress and helps it off my shoulders, she whispers, "You make a beautiful bride, Sammy Jo. Marcus is a lucky man."

"He is." There's a part of me that yearns for things to be different. For this to be a real wedding and to feel the love. I wonder what Marcus is thinking right now and why did he bring my parents here when he knew I was going it alone?

Just the sweet gestures and the thoughtful acts of the past two days, makes my eyes fill up with hopeful tears. He may be distant most of the time, but when it matters, he's always there, surprising me with a kind thought and sweet actions and this is just another of those.

"What did he tell you, mum?"

I'm interested to know and she strokes my hair with her fingers like Marcus apparently likes to do and she says wistfully, "He told me you met on the cruise and he couldn't live without you and somehow you agreed to marry him. He promised he would always care for you and to trust him on that. He told us both not to worry and even though this was fast, too fast really, it would always have happened regardless of time and he asked for our blessing because it would mean everything to you both."

"Are you angry?" I can't think about the lies Marcus told them just to get them here and bite my lip as I wait for the telling off, I'm sure I deserve."

"I'm never angry with you, Sammy Jo because you can do no wrong in my eyes. I just want to be here for you, we both do and we always will be."

She laces my fingers with hers and we share a moment. Mother and daughter experiencing something we hoped would come but never knew when that would be. The moment I supposedly grow into a woman myself and finally understand that secret when life comes together in the most exciting way.

Then why do I still feel as if I'm playing a part in a very complicated movie?

CHAPTER 26

Having my mum beside me has lifted my spirits, either that or the ones we've been consuming since breakfast. I feel on a high and it's not due to any drugs Mrs Everhard may have inadvertently slipped me either. I am swept away by the occasion because tomorrow is my wedding day.

Florrie smiles across the table and mouths the words, "Are you ok?"

Nodding, I raise my glass to hers. "You'll look beautiful, Florrie. That pink dress really suits your colouring."

She nods with enthusiasm. "Yes, it was a toss-up between that one or the one with the huge split up the side. I'm guessing Jake would have preferred that, but I feel happier with the one I've chosen."

"Is that your colour scheme darling, pink and white?"

Mum looks interested and I feel ashamed to admit I haven't got a clue.

Camilla jumps in and says with excitement, "Yes, the roses are blooming lovely at the moment and I have instructed my gardener to prepare them for a floral display of the most extravagant kind."

I stare at her in horror, imagining the rose garden massacre on my conscience. "Please don't sacrifice your garden for us. I'm sure some greenery from the hedgerows will be enough. I can't allow you to decimate your pride and joy."

"Oh, nonsense, darling." Camilla grins. "I have so many roses it won't even dent it. No, I love a good session of flower arranging and will spend a few happy hours when we return, making everything look amazing."

"Can I help?"

Florrie looks at her with interest because this is right up her street and Camilla looks delighted.

"Of course, I would love that."

Mum interrupts, "Me too, I love flower arranging." She looks almost apologetic. "You don't mind do you, Sammy Jo? I mean, we could all do it; that could be fun."

"Of course, count me in."

Just thinking of a pleasant afternoon in the church arranging flowers lifts my spirits a little. Maybe God will favour me with a miracle and make Marcus actually fall in love with me. I need all the help I can get and need to embrace my manifestation powers and make it happen.

When we leave the restaurant, it suddenly strikes me that we have a huge problem and I groan.

"What's the matter, darling? You're not sick, are you? Oh, my, I should have seen the signs. The flushed, distracted look, the fact you've been so quiet, you're coming down with something, aren't you?" Camilla looks so worried I must look like a character from the Walking Dead and I feel slightly concerned about that as I say with a sigh, "I can't drink and drive."

The fact we've been knocking back the spirits all morning

has obviously distracted my brain from remembering I'm the designated driver and there is no way of getting home.

Florrie groans. "I completely forgot about that. What are we going to do?"

"It's fine, I'll call one of the boys, not Marcus, of course, we're keeping him well away from you, darling, for tradition's sake."

"I thought that only included the night before."

I feel strangely disappointed that I won't be seeing him until I meet him at the altar and wonder if this is such a good idea. For some reason, I'm having crazy second thoughts. It's all too much and I need reassuring that I'm doing the right thing. Without him by my side to remind me, I'm liable to panic because this feels so cold, so business-like, and I don't feel anything like I wanted to on the day before my wedding.

Left on my own, I'll panic. Wallow in self-loathing and doubts about where the bunnies will live. Their homes will be destroyed just because I'm lusting after a man who has given me an opportunity to spend time with him. I don't deserve a nice wedding with everyone helping me like this. I deserve nothing because this marriage is a sham and Marcus, me and God know it.

Camilla is talking earnestly on the phone and breathes a sigh of relief. "Dom said he will come. He'll bring Brad with him and he'll drive your car back, Sammy, or something like that."

I'm not sure how I feel about that and just smile. Dom hates me. I chose his brother over him and in doing so, he stands to lose everything. The house, the land, and the dream of keeping everything the same. I wouldn't put it past him to kidnap me, or something along those lines. I'm just grateful mum and Florrie are nearby. Yes, I'll stick with them and then nothing can possibly happen.

"Maybe we should grab a coffee and wait?" Ever practical,

Florrie points to a sweet little coffee shop across the street and Camilla smiles.

"Probably for the best, I'm seeing two of you right now, which won't be beneficial when I festoon the church with floral abundance."

Linking her arm in Florrie's, they head off slightly unsteady on their feet and mum laughs. "Camilla's lovely, Sammy. You know, when Marcus called and told us, I imagined all sorts. I was afraid for you but meeting him and now his mother makes me happier. I'm just a little hurt you never trusted me with this."

Now I feel bad again and sigh. "I didn't want you to judge me and try to talk me out of it because I'd made up my mind. I know it's fast, way too fast, but I want this, mum."

She stares at me for a long time and then sighs. "I'm sorry to say this but I will have failed in my duty as a mother unless I have this conversation."

Standing in the middle of the street in Riverton is probably not the best place for a heart to heart, but I nod and resign myself to a lot of disappointed words heading my way.

"Go on."

She sounds so sad, I wonder if I've broken her and she whispers, "I just wish we had the opportunity to do this the way I always wanted. It appears your life is on fast forward, and I was so distracted, I missed that. I thought we would have years of planning an engagement party, many days like this one where we would exhaust every wedding dress shop in the county. Attend bridal fairs and plan cars and flowers. I had it all worked out and I suppose I'm grieving for that now because I feel like a guest at my own daughter's wedding and am just going along with someone else's idea of what that should be like."

I feel so bad. It's as if she's cut my heart out and left me bleeding to death on the streets of Riverton. I've disappointed her in the worst possible way and then she heaps more agony on me by saying sadly, "Are you pregnant? Is that why you're in such a hurry?"

Instinctively my hand flutters to my stomach and I gasp, "No, of course not."

Just imagining what that would have involved makes me wish I was, but no, Marcus has no desire for me in that department, which is probably a very good thing, anyway.

Mum looks worried. "What is it then? Are you sick? Please tell me no."

"No."

I take her hand and squeeze it gently. "I just…" Can I lie to her again to put her heart at rest? To make her believe this farce knowing my divorce in two years' time will sadden her and act as one big I told you so? The fact I've denied her everything she wanted makes me feel like the worst possible daughter alive and I feel so low right now, I could curl up into a puddle of tears in the road and pray for an end to a very different beginning.

"Sammy, do you want a latte and what about you Dora?"

Florrie shouts across the street and we both say in unison, "Latte, please."

We share a look and mum smiles. "We always were close, Sammy. Thought the same, wanted the same things, laughed at the same jokes. I suppose that's what hurts the most. I thought we were better than this."

"I'm sorry, mum." My words don't mean a thing because I know in agreeing to help Marcus, I have sacrificed my own integrity and broken my parent's hearts in the process. Was it worth it? I already know the answer to that because nothing is worth causing the people who love you the most, this unbearable heartache.

It's not too late to stop this, change your mind, leave and never come back.

That little voice inside my head is always there, reminding me I still have a choice.

As we walk across the street to join the others, it plays around my mind like a song that just won't go away.

Maybe I should listen to it, restore some of my mother's faith in me, admit I've made the biggest mistake of my life, and cut my losses.

As Camilla laughs at something Florrie whispers in her ear, I envy them the close relationship that is already forming. It's because Florrie is here for the right reasons and has found her happily ever after. Mine is a sham, a pretence, and my heart is heavy as I deal with the repercussions of that.

I know my mum is concerned about me. I can sense it from her straight back and frozen expression. This is what I'd hoped to avoid and I can't believe Marcus took it upon himself to go against my wishes.

CHAPTER 27

Half an hour later, Camilla looks up and sighs with relief.

"There they are."

I blink when I see the camper van heading our way and Florrie laughs out loud. "This is fun. I've never been in one of these, unlike my friend here."

She nudges me as I endure some kind of post-traumatic stress episode at the sight of it and cringe as Florrie laughs, "The dogging wagon, that's what Jake calls it, anyway."

"Oh no darling, we don't have dogs. Brad only keeps it to entertain his young ladies up at Pineland Forest. Much better than the back seat of a car, wouldn't you agree?" Camilla looks thoughtful, but mum looks absolutely horrified and I shrink a little under the disapproval in her gaze as Florrie laughs.

"You'd know all about that, wouldn't you, Sammy? Jake told me Facebook was lit up with a video of you and Marcus being arrested the other night along with all the others. I haven't laughed so much in my life at the sight of you standing there with 'sexy babe' written all over you."

I can only imagine the alcohol has lowered her filter because the look on my mum's face will live with me to my dying day.

"Arrested! What's this all about, Sammy? What have you done? Does it involve dogs? Oh, please say it doesn't. Are you involved in something – shady?"

Mum looks as if she's about to hyperventilate and Camilla laughs out loud. "I asked Brad if I could borrow it when I meet my next date from Executive Escorts then I could see what all the fuss is about."

Mum's head swivels like a barn owl as she turns to stare at Camilla in horror and Florrie starts giggling at the thought of Camilla in the dogging wagon, as it is fondly known as.

I don't even have time to explain; not that I'm relishing the thought of that, anyway, before a loud honk makes just about everyone in Riverton look up as Brad screeches to a halt and beside him, looking slightly irritated, is Dom.

"Ladies, ladies, allow me to come to your rescue."

Brad grins as Camilla shrieks, "Brad, thank goodness! I don't suppose you have any champagne on ice in that wagon of yours. I'm a little dry, you know?"

She wobbles precariously on her feet and Brad slings his arm around his mother's shoulders and says fondly, "I think Marcus and Sammy polished that off the other night, but I have some brandy – for medicinal purposes, of course."

"Lovely, darling, lead me to water and I shall drink."

Camilla is supported by her incorrigible son as Florrie runs after them. "Me too." Leaving me caught between a rock and a hard place as I'm flanked on both sides by my furious mother and an equally furious Dom.

Mum just says icily, "I think you have some more explaining to do, young lady. Prepare to tell me everything."

She storms off after the others and I don't know where I

would rather be right now as Dom holds out his hand and says coolly, "Your keys."

Fumbling in my bag, I hand them over with shaking fingers and he sighs. "We need to talk."

"We do?" I stare anxiously at the dogging wagon, wondering which is the lesser of the two evils and decide Dom is a much better bet than my mother right now and say with a sigh, "I'll ride with you. It is my car, after all. You are insured to drive it, aren't you?"

That has only just occurred to me, and he nods. "My insurance covers me for any car, so hop in."

It feels strange being a passenger in my own car and as I buckle up, he adjusts the seat with a growl. "For goodness's sake, why is this seat so close to the wheel? You're not that small, surely."

"I like it that way." I feel annoyed that he's calling me out on something that is surely my business in my own car and I say sharply, "Anyway, it's my car, my rules."

We watch the camper van squeal off into the distance and we follow at a more leisurely pace, which gives me time to adjust to the morning I've had already. I'm quite glad of the alcoholic haze surrounding me as it dulls the fear of what Dom is going to say.

"I'm sorry, Sammy."

I think I must have misheard him and say in surprise. "What did you say?"

"I'm sorry." He sighs. "If you must know, I'm not feeling very proud about my behaviour concerning you and it was wrong of me to make you feel bad about your decision."

"Why the change of heart?" I'm confused, and he laughs, which surprises me more than anything because the hard edge he wears so well is softening and for the first time since I came here, I relax a little in his company.

"The thing is, I would have done anything to beat Marcus to that inheritance out of spite."

That doesn't make me feel any better actually because it reinforces the fact, he was using me too.

"What's changed then?" I am definitely interested to know, and he shrugs. "Marcus knocked some sense into me."

Picturing Marcus beating seven bells out of his brother shocks me a little as I imagine a brawl behind closed doors and I say, sounding rather shocked, "He hit you."

Dom laughs, and it lightens the atmosphere a little.

"No, metaphorically actually, but he made me see the error of my ways where it concerns you."

"Oh."

I'm not sure what on earth is going on and he says in a kinder tone. "If it's any consolation, I think you'll be good together."

"Why do you say that?" I can't believe what I'm hearing because Dom knows only too well the circumstances of this marriage, and he grins. "Because you already are."

Wishing I was sipping brandy in the van with the others, I'm confused to see what's changed and Dom says a little wistfully, "I hope it works out."

"I'm guessing it will." Thinking of Marcus getting the land and his development makes that a pretty sure thing, and Dom interrupts my thoughts by saying, "I envy you both. What started out as a crazy scheme has ended well for everyone involved."

"It has?" I'm not sure if I meant that as a question, or confirmation, but I'm thinking it hasn't worked that well for me so far. I'm still doubting if it's the right thing for Dream Valley and what about my heart? It's currently in critical mode because I've only got until tomorrow to change my own mind and stop something that should never have started.

"So, what did Marcus say exactly?" I really need to know what miracle sentences he constructed to change Dom's mind.

"He agreed to scale down his plans."

"In what way?"

"The development. He agreed it was probably in Dream Valley's best interests to ring-fence a nature reserve around it. Plant some trees, encourage the wildlife into their new home and offer a more sustained environment. He wants to build with that in mind and incorporate solar and natural energy, reducing the carbon emissions and saving money for the people who live there. I couldn't argue with that because it's the right thing to do."

"It is." My eyes fill with tears once again because the rabbits will have a home. I wonder if we can somehow make it bunny paradise and I would love to be involved in the planning of that.

Dom laughs softly. "To be honest, it's done me a huge favour because I never really wanted the house and land, anyway."

"You didn't." I'm shocked and he grins.

"It was always the business for me. I used to go with my dad on weekends and holidays. I loved spending time at the office and the warehouses. I loved the industry, I always have and if I get my way, I'll be in charge of them, as soon as I have a wedding ring on my finger, that is."

"So, what's your plan?" I'm interested because Marcus has obviously handed the baton to his brother in this relay race against time, and I'm wondering how long he has to run.

"I'm in no hurry, though. Luckily, I am running the business now anyway, and that will only change if my brothers decide they want it too."

"I thought…"

"Yes, Brad wants the money and Jake the shares. I don't

think that's changed, so it appears my father will be turning in his grave because none of us are in a hurry to sign on the dotted line."

"So, you can do things the old-fashioned way and fall in love. That must feel good."

I hate that I sound wistful, jealous even and Dom hesitates before saying, "It could work out for you, stranger things have happened."

"Maybe."

Injecting a little enthusiasm in my voice, I'm glad that we've sorted this out. I hated that he was angry with us both and am glad at least this is the last Hudson brother whose marriage will be a sham.

Shame it's also my marriage, but I knew that from the moment Marcus asked me.

We soon turn into Valley House and catching sight of the huge white box in the back of my car, may as well be a gigantic red flag because why am I such a fool? Compromising my principles and my integrity for a crazy scheme that wasn't needed, anyway. Maybe Marcus will back out now he's settled things with his brother. I wouldn't be surprised and far from making things better, Dom appears to have made me feel a hundred times worse.

CHAPTER 28

Thank goodness for Camilla Hudson. As soon as we arrived at Valley House, she adopted my mother and spirited her away to settle into her room, giving me some much-needed breathing space.

Florrie is a little worse for wear and groans as she puts her head in her hands as she sits on the edge of my bed – or I should say, Marcus's bed.

"I wish I hadn't drunk so much. I've got such a headache coming on."

"I've got some Nurofen in my bag."

Rifling through it, I hand her the packet and she grabs a bottle of water from beside the bed and chugs it down with a deep sigh.

"Now I just need to wait for the magic to work."

"Florrie…"

She looks up sharply, "What?"

"What should I do?"

"About…"

"The wedding, Marcus, life actually."

"Are you having second thoughts?" That's grabbed her

attention and I lie beside her and put the pillow over my face, mumbling, "A little."

She tears it away and looks down at me with concern, and I shrug. "I mean, having mum here makes everything more real. Just seeing the hurt in her eyes was like a painful blow to my heart and I haven't even seen my dad yet. What if he looks at me the same way? Then there's the rest of my family. My brother, my grandparents, aunts and uncles. Word will get out and they will all think I'm pregnant and racing against time amid a scandal of epic proportions. Maybe I should just leave. Admit I'm an idiot and save myself from complete humiliation for the rest of my life."

"Is that what you want?"

Florrie sounds disappointed, probably because she likes having me here because she's more than happy about her own situation.

"No, not really."

"Then why think it?"

"Because..." *I do*

Once again, those words haunt me as I remember the reason for speaking them in the first place. I didn't want my family here to witness my shame because of one reason only. Marcus doesn't love me.

It's almost ridiculous to think he arranged them to come because of that conversation and, if it was, what does that mean for us? There is no way he does love me. Why would he? And I'm just clutching at an insane wish that he does.

A knock on the door interrupts our heart to heart and Florrie whispers, "We'll talk later, don't do anything rash."

As I jump off the bed, I say softly, "I already have."

Both mum and Camilla are waiting as I open the door and I shrink under the scrutiny of my mother's gaze as Camilla says in a slightly more sober voice, "Come on girls, the flowers need arranging."

We follow them out and my heart sinks as Brad waits for us by the van and grins. "It appears that I'm your designated driver today, ladies. All aboard the love bus."

Not daring to look at my mum, I clamber on board and shrink into the corner, wishing I could wake up from this obviously bad dream.

～

ONCE AGAIN, I find myself walking up the cobbled path to enlightenment as we head into St Thomas's and I look around for Reverend Bowers. He appears to be somewhere else and I'm glad about that as I look at the buckets of roses and foliage that have been left here by Camilla's gardener.

Ribbons and candles are also present and I feel a tingle of excitement as I contemplate transforming this ancient church into a modern-day fairy-tale.

Florrie almost falls on the buckets with a careless enthusiasm fuelled by alcohol and Camilla starts issuing instructions as we prepare to festoon this church in pink and white.

Camilla is tackling the huge pedestals on either side of the altar and Florrie is in charge of the window sills. Mum and I have been detailed with the rose-covered arch above the church door and as we head outside, I suppose this is a good time for the chat she is intent on having.

Working beside her, despite the circumstances, is a very pleasant experience, and she appears to have lost a little of the edge she left the town with.

"This is so pretty, Sammy. Camilla has exquisite taste."

"She does." I look at the pretty blooms, delicate and sweet-smelling, mixing with white cow parsley and gypsophila. Beautiful white hydrangeas act as filler and as we work putting everything in place, I can't remember a time better spent.

Mum laughs and shakes her head.

"What's so funny?"

"You are."

"That's a little rude, I can't help it you know." I grin as she giggles. "Florrie filled me in on your night in the forest on the way back from town. I must say, I would have loved to see your face when you were standing among sexual people."

"Sexual people, what on earth is that supposed to mean?" I bite down my own giggle as she whispers, in case God is listening, "I never knew things like that existed. I thought it was something to do with actual dogs but Florrie told me – well I think you can guess."

"So, you're not angry then?"

"No, not really."

She says with a sigh. "The thing is, I'm still wrapping my head around it all. To be honest, it's been a bit of a shock but I'm adjusting it to it now."

"You are?" Thanking my friend from the bottom of my heart, she appears to have worked a miracle on my mother and I relax a little.

"You see, Sammy Jo, like I said before, this has been my dream for a very long time, before you were even born. As a young girl, I always imagined my own daughter's wedding day. It's a little different to how I imagined it but I've been thinking."

"Ok." Taking a deep breath, I prepare myself for the worst and she says with a giggle, "We will do it all over again."

"What?" She nods vigorously. "Yes, we won't say anything to anyone and start planning our own big day as soon as possible. Then we will pretend it's the first time and you can wear your dress again, Florrie too and everyone will be happy."

She looks thoughtful. "It will have to be soon, though. I mean, you never know, you may decide to start a family on your honeymoon. The dress wouldn't fit and we would have to accommodate a bump into the proceedings."

"Mum, please, one wedding at a time, I'm begging you."

My mind is buzzing because this is going from bad to worse and I can't even move my mind past tomorrow, let alone do it all over again. What on earth will Marcus think about that? He'll be irritated and think it a waste of time. Now I have a headache coming on and I start arranging roses and hydrangeas with a nervous energy powered by anxiety.

"AH, THERE SHE IS."

We both jump as the shouting vicar stands behind us and says loudly, "Just thought you should know, this is a listed building and we don't allow anything that will harm the structure. Make sure everything is easily removed, and no damage done. Church rules, I'm afraid."

"Of course," I share a look with my mother and say quickly, "Um, Reverend Bowers, this is my mother, Dora Miles."

"Pleased to meet you, madam and on such a happy occasion. This might be the best moment to mention no confetti in the churchyard. Can I leave it with you to spread the word? Church rules, I'm afraid."

"Of course." Mum looks a little bewildered as he says loudly, "Maybe we should have that run through now. I mean, it's scheduled for later, but I have a death to attend and need to reschedule."

"A death."

Mum doesn't how to react and he nods. "Joseph Pebbles, he died this morning at the grand old age of ninety-six."

"I'm sorry to hear that." Mum voices her sympathy and he nods. "Yes, terrible business, really. It was a heart attack brought on by a very indecent episode in the care home. I wouldn't be surprised if there were more causalities when word gets out."

"What happened?" Mum is riveted by his story and I share her interest because what could have possibly happened in the care home to cause such a scandal?

He lowers his voice to normal levels and says, looking around him, "He was having an affair with another resident. A bit of a shock but what a way to go, hey."

He winks and looks at the half-dressed arch of roses with admiration.

"Super job. Maybe I can call on your support for the harvest festival. Mrs Somerville is a little stuck in her ways and can't see past wheat and chaff. I'll expect to see you at the organising committee. It will be fun."

My heart sinks as I anticipate being roped into just about every voluntary job going and pray that I find the courage from somewhere to say no for once in my life. It's that inability that got me in this position in the first place, and it appears I will never learn and always be running away from my actions because I can't face my decisions.

"There's my girl."

A familiar voice has me dropping my secateurs and running, because coming up the cobbled pathway is my father, accompanied by Jake. He holds out his arms and I fall into them and can't help but sob on his shoulder as everything comes to boiling point.

As his arms lock around me and wrap me in familiarity, I cry in his arms in the vain hope he can somehow make this all better.

"She's a little emotional, Rod." My mother rubs my back and I can only imagine the knowing looks they are sharing right now, and Jake coughs nervously. "Um. I'll just, um, head inside, you know, Florrie, mum, well…"

He heads off awkwardly and my dad pulls away and says with concern. "What's the matter? You should be jumping for joy? Why the tears?"

"I'm sorry, dad."

"Hush, darling, you have nothing to be sorry about, in my case, anyway. I'm here now and looking forward to offloading you to another. I'm rejoicing right now."

Laughing through my tears, I love that he's here because he's always had an ability to make everything alright.

Sniffing, I smile and take his hand. "It's good to see you, dad."

"You too, princess."

Mum points towards the archway. "We should carry on. Maybe you can help, Rod."

"Probably not, but I just wanted to check on you both before Jake takes me for a pint at the Blue Balls."

"The what?"

Dad laughs at the horror on mum's face. "The pub, Dora. Strange choice of name but all that concerns me is they serve cold beer and possibly a few pork scratchings."

"Typical." Mum rolls her eyes. "The men take to the pub while the women do all the work. Where have you been until now, anyway?"

"A suit fitting and a chat with my new son-in-law."

I look up sharply as mum says with interest, "What did he say?"

Dad just winks. "All the right things. Anyway, don't let me keep you. I have things to do. Apparently, we have a nice dinner arranged tonight at a place called The Last Resort."

My heart sinks as he carries on. "Then it's an early night before the big day tomorrow. I must say, I never really knew what to expect after that surprising phone call yesterday, but I've been pleasantly surprised. You did well, love. Marcus is a good chap and I'm happy to give you away to him."

"Don't be ridiculous, Rod, you're not giving Sammy away, if anything, you're just gaining a son, which reminds me your own one called me this morning and said he can't make it."

"Ryan knows." I feel dizzy as I think about my brother now knowing what a fool his sister is and once again, I could murder Marcus for dragging my entire family into this mess with me. "Don't worry, darling." Mum smiles. "He'll be at the next one."

"The next one." Dad looks absolutely horrified and mum says with a determination that usually gets her what she wants, "I'll tell you all about it later, Rod. I've had an amazing idea that will help us navigate this disaster and save face with our family and friends. All is good."

Disaster. Just hearing her describe my upcoming wedding just about sums it all up. A disaster waiting to happen and I appear to be heading for a very big fall.

CHAPTER 29

It appears that Marcus and his brothers are spending the night in a hotel in Riverton, and I'm not sure if I'm happy about that or not. Keeping to tradition, I haven't seen him since breakfast and I miss him, which surprises me a little. Everything is happening around me and yet there is only one thing I want. Him.

It's extremely doubtful he thinks the same of me, but just the tingle I get when I think of him tells me I'm going nowhere but down that aisle at a brisk pace before he changes his mind.

I can't help myself. Despite everything, I want him. I want to be his wife, but it's the divorce part I'm not looking forward to. It was always my plan to make him fall in love with me, but is that really an option when I've pandered to every thought in his head. I'm not sure he even respects me. I wouldn't because I appear to have no mind of my own and as I get ready for my last night of freedom, once again I consider the option of calling a cab and heading home with my tail between my legs.

Mind you, it would be just my luck to get Jim Burrows

and his tractor driving skills and Marcus would gently stroll alongside my great escape and persuade me to stay by saying all the right things. Isn't that how dad described their conversation and I don't doubt it for a second. Marcus always knows exactly the right thing to say, which is why he's so skilled at manipulation.

Deciding on a yellow silk dress that dances just above my knees, I grab a small denim jacket to keep the chill off and curl my hair to give it some bounce. I feel quite good about my appearance, but inside I'm fighting a losing battle. I'm so conflicted because my head is having a massive argument with my heart and it's exhausting.

I meet the others who have met in the living room and Camilla looks so lovely in a white silk pant suit with her hair piled on top of her head. So elegant and yet understated and as I smile, she gives me a twirl and says loudly, "I can't wear white tomorrow, no matter how much I wanted to turn up in one of those gorgeous dresses of Mrs Everhards, this is the next best thing. I hope you don't mind."

Hugging her on impulse, I grin. "Wear whatever you like, it's as much your day as ours."

Mum looks smart in her red shift dress and matching pumps and I hug her too, whispering, "You look lovely, mum."

"Thanks, you don't look so bad yourself."

Florrie claps her hands with excitement. "This is going to be so much fun."

I look around and notice my dad is missing and my mum whispers, "Your father was invited to the hotel. I think there's some kind of stag do going on. I despatched him to keep an eye on things; you never know, these things have a habit of getting out of hand and he needs to step up and take charge in the absence of their father."

Just thinking about the Hudson brothers let loose in

Riverton, probably in Brads' dogging wagon, makes my heart sink. Of course, they will take full advantage of this and I expect Marcus will be out of control, making the most of his last night of freedom. I take some consolation from the fact he's not heading to The Olive Tree and Maria won't be the glad recipient of his attention tonight. Imagining elastic tie girl already giving him a lap dance makes me weary and I say with a fake smile, "Maybe we should go."

We head off in my car because I have promised I'm never drinking again because I need to keep a cool head and even when Camilla insisted she'd pay for a cab, I had to decline because knowing Jim we would probably miss my own wedding at the speed he drives.

∼

THE OLIVE TREE is lit up like a Christmas tree with fairy lights covering the frontage and two bay trees standing proudly either side of the door. In contrast to how it looks during the day, it almost seems magical tonight, and I've always been a sucker for anything with fairy lights. In fact, I intend on decorating my entire house in them because nothing gives you an inner glow and a sense of satisfaction than a well-placed string of fairy lights.

We crowd through the door and my heart sinks as I immediately catch the eye of Maria, who is not looking so happy to see us. However, as soon as Camilla steps forward, she is all smiles and gushes, "Mrs Hudson, I am so pleased to see you, you look amazing, then again you always do."

Florrie nudges me and pulls a face and I relax a little. Yes, I have my best friend by my side and that gives me a certain kind of strength. In fact, I can only go through with this because of her. She has always been there for me and the same for me. When her bridegroom turned out to be married already, I stepped into his shoes and took care of her. I never left her side and gave everything up to sail away and help mend her broken heart. It's funny how good comes out of misery sometimes because if he hadn't turned out to be such a waste of time, we wouldn't be here now. Florrie wouldn't have met Jake and I wouldn't have met Marcus.

Pushing away the niggling voice in my head that thinks it wouldn't have been such a bad thing, I follow the others to a table set in the corner and hear Maria say airily, "I don't usually allow hen parties out of respect for my other customers. They are too rowdy normally, but as it's you, Mrs Hudson, I have made a very welcome exception to the rule."

Camilla nods happily, "Call me Camilla, darling, and you are so kind. I can't promise we won't be rowdy, goodness if we're not I would consider it the ultimate failure, but we'll be respectful of your other diners. You don't need to worry about that."

We take our seats and almost before my back hits the chair rest, Florrie whips out a sash from nowhere and drapes it around me. Looking down at the pink creation, I see 'Bride to be' in bold pink letters. Then she hands one to each of them, 'mother of the bride,' 'mother of the groom' and 'bridesmaid' for her.

"Lovely, darling." Camilla looks more than happy about hers and mum looks a little embarrassed but smiles and throws me a wink.

Camilla claps her hands as the waitress heads over and says loudly, "A bottle of your finest champagne please."

Florrie laughs under her breath, "One of many tonight if Camilla gets her way."

"I'm not drinking, I need to drive."

"Nonsense, darling." Camilla listens in and waves her hand. "I'll call a cab. You must drink on your hen night. It's the law."

My heart sinks because I'd rather never drink again if I had to call Jim's taxi, but hopefully Camilla won't notice if I stick to water tonight.

Despite how I feel about the woman in charge of The Olive Tree, the food is good and we are soon tucking into dough balls and appetisers as if we haven't eaten for weeks.

Camilla is in her element and waves at people she knows like the queen and I suppose she is – the Queen of Dream Valley. I know the Hudson's play a very important role here. They live in the biggest house and are integral to the running of it. The fact there are four eligible bachelors in town makes them a target of extreme interest and I expect I'll have to get used to the scrutiny being one of them brings.

I don't miss the surreptitious glances that head my way from the other interested diners. It's like living in a fish tank, feeling the fascination from onlookers as if we are exotic specimens to admire. But I'm not one of them and probably never will be and I can imagine those stares turning ones of pity when I pack my bags and leave a single woman once more.

I've never really understood that saying, 'alone in a crowd' until now. Everyone around me is having an amazing time and seems to have life all worked out. I should be the happiest one here, but I'm not. I am wrestling with my conscience so badly because I am lying to myself as much as everyone around me. I think I can pull this off and actually make Marcus fall in love with me, but what if I can't?

The fact I haven't seen him all day and so much has happened, increases the distance between us. I picture him enjoying his last night of freedom by drinking and flirting, with probably a stripper or two thrown in for good measure. I expect he's enjoying every minute of it and why not. He owes me nothing. He is still that single man with everything going for him, and I will have to accept that he's not mine to enjoy.

Sighing, I push back from my seat and say quickly, "Excuse me, I'm just heading to the ladies. I won't be long."

They all nod and then continue with their excited chatter as I head for a time out that I badly need.

I weave my way through the tables and smile at a few curious stares, and I'm not sure if it's because I apparently starred in a sex video on Facebook. Maybe this is what my life will be from now on, filmed at my worst and shared with the masses, just out of a morbid sense of fascination with the Hudson family.

Unfortunately, Maria follows me into the ladies, which doesn't really surprise me because I got the vibes from her very early on that she doesn't approve of me and I steel myself for more digs heading my way.

"Excuse me." She stops me from disappearing into a nearby cubicle to escape her and I sigh inside but fix a bright smile on my face.

"Yes."

"I um…"

She falters a little and looks a bit nervous and I wait for something I probably won't like hearing.

"It's well, I think you should know this."

CHAPTER 30

My heart is beating so fast inside me, I almost expect to see it diving through the window and galloping down the high street, rather than stand and face whatever she's about to say.

For a moment she looks unsure, a little vulnerable even, and time seems to pass extremely slowly as we both wait for whatever she has to say.

"Before Marcus went on the cruise, the actual night before, he um, well, he spent the night with me."

I had kind of guessed their relationship went a lot deeper than he pretended, but I wasn't expecting the crashing blow to my heart that leaves me reeling.

I just stare as she says with a slight edge to her voice. "The Hudson boys are such candy to the girls around here. Brad dishes his favours around like confetti, the others not so much. They have a reputation largely because of Brad, but Marcus has always been a tough nut to crack, never really playing the game and putting all his energy into building up his business. So…"

She looks uncomfortable, but I'm not in the right frame

of mind to make her feel better about this and just stare at her with a frozen look as I try to deal with what this means for me.

"Maybe he lowered his guard. I'm not sure why, but we got talking in a bar in Riverton the night before they left. I couldn't believe my luck because he was actually talking to me. He was never interested before and I suppose I was flattered, hopeful for something more and, well, you can probably guess the rest. Then I woke up in my flat beside an empty bed and felt like such a fool. He left before I even knew it, with no note, no text or explanation. All day I waited and only found out they had left when someone snapped a picture of them leaving at the airport. You see, that's what living with the Hudson's is like, as I'm sure you've already found out."

Thinking of the video on Facebook, I know exactly what that's like and I feel any animosity I have towards this woman, slipping away with every word she speaks.

She looks nervous, a little embarrassed and as if she's in two minds whether to tell me this or not and I feel sorry for her really and my heart is hardening against my soon to be husband.

She sighs and looks worried. "The thing is, when I saw you holding hands that day in here, I was angry he never acknowledged me or what we'd done. He didn't call when he returned home, not even a text. It was as if he wanted to wipe the whole thing from his mind and then he announced he was engaged."

I feel so bad for her and for me because I don't like the picture she is painting of the man I supposedly love.

"Then there's his father."

Startled, I look at her in dismay because surely, she didn't… She shakes her head. "Anthony Hudson was a rogue. A cheating rogue who never deserved Camilla. She stood by him through every scandal thrown her way and it's not surprising she's enjoying her freedom now he's gone. Which brings me to the reason I followed you in here."

Her eyes glitter with unshed emotion and she takes a deep breath as she whispers, "I wanted to warn you. To show you what you're getting into. The Hudson men, well, they are more like their father than I'd feel comfortable with. I have no other reason than I would hate knowing this and then watch the same thing happen to you."

"Thank you." My voice is weak, but the resolve in me is growing stronger. "I appreciate it."

She nods and the slight tremble to her bottom lip makes me feel so angry with Marcus. I never had him down as a one-night stand sort of guy and the disgust must show in my face because she flinches as if I've hit her.

"Please don't think I do that all the time, Sammy. I don't, which is why it's been so hard. I suppose it was because I had my opportunity with the brother nobody can ever seem to crack. I always fancied Marcus, most women do, but I really wanted him to notice me and now I wish I hadn't bothered because he moved on and left me feeling used and rather foolish. Please don't be me, Sammy. Stand up to him and insist on better. You need to show Marcus Hudson that he can't always call the shots and that people have actual feelings. Anyway…"

She sighs as if a huge weight has shifted and smiles. "Do with that little speech what you will. I've done what I thought was right and I'm sorry if you hate me for that. Despite everything, I do hope it works out, for you, anyway."

As she turns to leave, I reach out and stop her and she looks worried when she turns. Smiling, I whisper, "Thanks, Maria. I really appreciate it and if it's any consolation, I'm sorry."

"Thank you."

As she leaves, I feel even worse than I did before and I'm thinking of Marcus a little differently now. I kind of guessed that's what they were like, but hearing about it is a very different thing entirely.

It's some time before I make it back to the others and if anyone could have seen me perched on the toilet in the cubicle, with my head in my hands, they would have wondered what on earth was going on. But I was destroyed. I am destroyed because how can I possibly go through with this now? Everything is pointing to this being a very bad decision and I feel as if I'm drowning. Maybe I do need a shot of alcohol to steady my nerves. Is this the moment I become that woman? The one who is so unhappy she seeks comfort in the bottle while her husband does what the hell he likes?

The future doesn't look so rosy now, more distorted as I contemplate viewing the world from the bottom of a glass from now on.

All it will take is a moment of strength to prove to myself that I'm better than this.

Feeling conflicted, upset and so let down, I head back to the others with my brave face firmly plastered on.

～

"There she is." Florrie calls out with excitement and I smile with a bravery I don't feel inside.

"What have I missed?"

"Nothing yet." Florrie grins and I'm guessing she has something planned because she never could keep a secret.

Suddenly, a commotion by the door makes me look up and I see three firemen heading inside. The whole restaurant looks surprised and a little nervous as one of them says loudly, "Sammy Jo Miles."

My heart drops and I try to shrink back in my seat as Camilla yells, "Here she is."

Every eye in the place is looking at me right now, as well as several phones pointing in my direction. I want to die.

The three men head my way and out of nowhere, the theme tune to Magic Mike starts up and as they surround me, I know exactly what comes next.

Whipping off their helmets, I'm spun to face one of them as he stands astride me and starts unbuttoning his jacket.

Camilla is out of control, screaming with excitement as one of the others does the same to her and the look on my mum's face is worth it as one of them pulls her face towards his pelvis and grinds against her.

Florrie appears to be filming this and is giggling like mad and as the strippers begin their routine, I wish I was anywhere but here.

This could go down as one of the most embarrassing moments of my life, but thinking of Marcus probably doing exactly the same thing makes my heart harden and I toss my inhibitions out there for grabs.

Making the most of this, I smile and laugh and play up to the camera because I will not let Marcus think he's calling all the shots. I'm an independent woman who can make her own choices in life and so I'm ashamed to admit, I take full advantage of this and give back as good as I get because after all, these men are surely every woman's fantasy and I may as well indulge mine for a while.

CHAPTER 31

I am officially going to Hell. Waking up the morning after the night before is the purest agony. Despite my intentions, I drank more than the rest of them put together and ended the night dancing on every table in The Olive Tree with a very willing bridesmaid by my side. The fact Camilla was lap dancing one of the strippers made for entertaining pictures and even my mother let her hair down and polished off a bottle of champagne all to herself, while sitting on one of the stripper's knees, telling him her life story.

I can't even think about how many videos are probably premiering on Facebook at this moment and the fact my head is thumping like a very bad nightclub track makes me regret every moment of the night before.

Florrie groans beside me. "What time is it?"

"I don't have a clue."

"What day is it even?"

"Judgement day." I groan as I place the pillow over my face and say roughly, "Just kill me now."

"What, and leave me to face this alone? No way, babe, you're going nowhere."

"Stop talking."

Another voice comes from down the end of the bed and I feel a kick in my side as Camilla groans. "What time did we make it back?"

"3 am." The voice beside her sounds a little brighter than the rest and I pull myself up and look at my mother, who is tailing Florrie, beside Camilla."

"Why did we think this sleepover was such a good plan?"

I shake my head as my partners in crime stir from their pits with extreme hangovers.

"Our rooms were too far away."

Camilla looks bleary-eyed and puts her hand to her head. "How long did that cab take? I swear we left at 2 am. Did he get lost or something?"

"Remembering Jim arriving to collect us, I try to push away the image where I kissed him full on the lips and declared him a life saver."

Florrie groans again. "Did I really fire off three rounds into the air with an air rifle last night? Please tell me I dreamt that."

"No, that was you. I think you found it under the passenger seat and wound the window down and told everyone to wake up."

We all stare at one another with shame burning from our eyes and I feel so sick I'm not sure if I can make it through the next hour, let alone the day.

Florrie rolls out of bed and hits the floor and actually crawls to the bathroom.

"I need a wee."

Camilla sighs and looks at her watch. "I should head back to my room and change."

The fact we are all still wearing our clothes from the

night before is not a pleasant feeling and mum yawns loudly and laughs softly. "I had fun though."

"Me too." Camilla smiles at her with a solidarity earned by women who have bonded over a shared experience, and I nod in agreement. "It was amazing, thank you."

As they shift out of bed, mum says with a little disbelief, "Are you really going to bring those strippers as your dates to the wedding?"

"Did I arrange that? Goodness me, whatever next?"

Remembering Camilla leaving, surrounded by the gorgeous men, I laugh. "You did I'm afraid, maybe they won't remember."

"Do you think?" Camilla looks upset about that and mum laughs. "I hope for your sake they remember. I'm pretty sure they were as drunk as we were at the end of it. I feel bad for the other customers though. It's never nice seeing a gathering get out of hand so badly."

"Me too." I feel doubly bad for Maria, both for her bad experience with Marcus and the fact we trashed her restaurant.

"We should send flowers to Maria wrapped in pound notes as compensation."

Camilla nods. "Leave it with me, darling, I'll make sure she's ok."

As she drags herself to the door, she turns and smiles. "I knew having daughters would be such fun. I'm looking forward to many more nights like that one, Sammy. I just want to say I'm so happy you are both here, and I can't wait to have another Mrs Hudson in the house. We should stick together, girl code and all that. Those boys won't know what's hit them."

She links arms with my mother and says loudly, "Let's go and freshen up and I'll see if Mrs Jenkins is ready with breakfast. Goodness, all that activity has made me ravenous, darling."

"I couldn't eat a thing." Florrie emerges, looking like death, making me smile. "Go and grab a nice hot shower, and you'll feel a lot better. I know I'm going to."

As she makes to leave, she has a thought and turns, looking a little worried. "Are you ok, Sammy? I mean, about today, the wedding, Marcus?"

The million-dollar question I don't really have an answer for, and I shrug. "I think so."

"But…"

"I'm fine. Go and sort yourself out, I'll be ok."

She smiles thinly and leaves and as the door closes softly behind her, I'm left with all my doubts crowding around me. I don't have long to rearrange them either because in a few hours' time I could be making the biggest decision of my life.

CHAPTER 32

I don't have time for a hangover. I don't have time to consider my options either, because suddenly Valley House is a hive of activity.

When I venture out from my room, jaded and anxious, I am greeted by the most amazing flower arrangements positioned all over the house. The air is scented with a heady perfume that cannot fail to lift even the most despondent spirits.

I take my seat at breakfast and wave away the buck's fizz and opt for the fresh orange juice instead and listen to the excited chatter of my partners in crime as they reminisce on a night of girls behaving badly.

Noticing my father isn't here, I worry about what happened on Marcus's stag do and whisper to mum, "Where's dad?"

"Still in the hotel with the boys, I believe. I'm not sure really but I got a text telling me he'd be back to walk you up the aisle."

She smiles and I try to mirror it, but the nerves are taking hold of me and I concentrate on focusing on every minute at a time as I contemplate how this day will end.

Camilla has arranged for a mobile hairdresser to make us all look beautiful and Florrie has agreed to do my make-up in return for a review online. Obviously, I would do that anyway, but it's good to know I will be left in her more than capable hands.

As we work hard to cover up the excesses of the night before and attack a packet of Nurofen between us, I finally feel like my former self as I stare into the mirror while Florrie fusses around me like a mother hen.

My own mother is having her hair done, which leaves the two of us alone for the first time today.

"Are you nervous, babe?"

Florrie concentrates on powdering my face and I nod. "Yes, I can't help it, I am."

"I'm not surprised."

"What would you do if you were me?"

"I wouldn't be in this position in the first place." She sighs. "Don't get me wrong, Marcus is seriously gorgeous and before I met Jake, I was interested myself, but this seems so cold somehow. I want the best for you. We all do, but this isn't a marriage, it's a business deal, so how can I be happy about that."

"On his part, yes, but it's more than that for me."

The pity in her eyes causes me to swallow hard, and she shakes her head. "Don't cry, babe, you'll ruin my finest work and set me off at the same time."

"It's hard not to. You see, I think I love Marcus."

"I know."

Florrie sounds upset for me and I wonder what Jake has said. Almost as if she can read my mind and I wouldn't put that past her, she says as an aside, "Jake told me that he'd never seen Marcus like this."

"Like what?"

"Infatuated was the word I think he used."

The brush sweeps across my eyelid and I say sadly, "He's playing a part, that's all."

"Are you sure about that? I mean, I've known him as long as you have and he can't take his eyes off you for a second when he thinks no one is looking."

"Rubbish, he prefers his phone. He won't stop looking at the damn thing for a second."

"I don't see that. I see the way his eyes light up when you smile at him. The way he watches you when you walk away. Maybe he is playing a good game, trying to make it seem believable, but if that was the case, why the camping trip and why bring your parents here against your wishes?"

"Who knows what runs through his mind? I certainly don't."

"I think he loves you, Sammy, but he can't find the words to tell you, so he does sweet things to show you instead."

A warm feeling spreads through me as I remember the lovely little gestures he's made since I've been here. The way he holds my hand and the kisses we share. The camping trip was both a disaster and a dream. He surprises me a lot, and yet I can't push Maria out of my head.

"He slept with Maria the night before the cruise."

Florrie holds her eye shadow palette in mid-air and her face drops. "He did, wow."

"Then he left when she was sleeping and blanked her. Even when we went to her restaurant, he pretended it was all one sided. Totally ignored her and cut her out."

Florrie looks as disgusted as I feel and she shakes her head. "She could be lying."

"I doubt it. She told me Marcus was like his father. They all are. Temptation follows them everywhere and everyone wants them. How can I argue with that because I'm the same? Whatever he wants, I'm happy to oblige, so I'm no different to the rest of them. One day when he gets what he wants, he'll blank me too. Cut me out of his life with no care and move onto his next business opportunity. Don't you think?"

She crouches before me and takes my hand, ironically the one where the huge engagement ring weighs me down. As she studies it, she whispers, "Maybe he's changed since he met you."

"Or maybe not. Then there's the land. You should see what he wants to do with it. It's impressive, noble even, but too much. You know..."

I shake my head and sigh. "Dom told me they had come to an arrangement. Marcus has agreed to build fewer houses and devote some land to a nature reserve. Dom has now backed off and is happy to let Marcus have the land. What do you think, a noble gesture or a calculated one? Now he has no one standing in his way and he can have it all."

"I think I'd give him the benefit of the doubt; you haven't heard his side of the story. Remember, Sammy, Dom wanted you for the exact same reason, and you chose Marcus. That must have wounded his pride a little."

"Then why is he suddenly happy for us? Nothing makes sense and I'm expected to go along with this sham of a marriage because he wants to claim his part of the estate."

Florrie sighs and carries on with my make-up. "Only you know what you want, Sammy. If it's Marcus, you will do it anyway. Love has the power to turn our brains into mush and allow us to do things no sane person would ever contemplate. Just ask yourself, how will you feel if you walk away? Will you feel happy and proud that you made a stand, or will you miss him and have regrets further down the line? Maybe this marriage isn't a sham, not on your part anyway, and perhaps you should have discussed this with Marcus before today."

She carries on making me beautiful and I think every argument against this marriage presents itself and is firmly shot down by my heart. It's as if it's formed a defence around it against any attack and is going there, anyway.

CHAPTER 33

Florrie looks amazing. Her pale pink dress complements her hair colour along with the flowers that twist in a ring on top of her head. A gorgeous bouquet sets the outfit off and the happiness in her eyes almost makes this feel real.

Beside her, Camilla stands, a vision in blue with a hat that could rival any at Ascot Ladies' Day. She's popped in before she heads to the church and her happiness is evident by the huge smile on her face as she hugs me and whispers, "Welcome to the family, darling. We will always look after you, you're a Hudson now."

Part of me wonders if I'll make it that far because I'm changing my mind at a thousand miles an hour and as I turn to mum, she looks so emotional I feel bad all over again as she whispers, "I'm so proud of you, Sammy; you look like an angel."

Then my dad walks in and just the look on his face causes the tears to spill and three horrified gasps fill the air. Florrie rushes forward with an emergency hanky as my father says with a thick voice, "You look beautiful, princess."

I can't argue with that because I *feel* beautiful. My hair has been curled and then heaped on top of my head with a tiara fixing the veil in place. Small flowers have been woven into the up-do making me feel like the princess he thinks I am. Silk underwear hugs my body and the dress I fell in love with feels like a second skin as it caresses my body like a proud lover and I have never felt as pretty as I'm feeling now.

Camilla sighs and then says regretfully, "I should go. My dates have turned up and we're needed at the church."

Florrie grins as mum shares a horrified look with my father and I can't resist giggling as I picture the vicar's face when Camilla Hudson walks into the church accompanied by three male strippers.

The room empties as everyone prepares to take their positions. Mum and Florrie are riding in a car to the church, something that Marcus has arranged, and I just hope it doesn't involve the dogging wagon or Jim Burrows.

As the door closes, my father steps forward and smiles. "How are you feeling?"

"Good thanks." My smile may be firm, but my nerves are shaking as my rash decision comes back to bite me with a vengeance.

"How was Marcus?"

Finally, I can ask someone the only thing I want to know and I look eagerly for a sign of disapproval from my father that would probably tilt my decision the other way.

Instead, he smiles like a proud father and grins. "I like him, Sammy, really like him. You know, he has surprised me – a lot and I think you've made the right decision."

"You do?" I'm surprised because ordinarily no man has ever been worthy in my father's eyes and I think this is the first time I've ever seen him approve of my choice.

"Why?" I'm burning to know and he shakes his head. "You'll see."

He holds out his arm and says with a huge amount of pride in his voice, "It's time, princess. Are you ready?"

Am I? I'm not so sure, but I smile and nod. "As I'll ever be."

As I take his arm and walk past the heady floral arrangements. Through the luxurious rooms of Valley House and out into the sunlight, it all feels as if it's happening to someone else. When I see the beautiful white limousine waiting for me, I blink in shock at the uniformed driver holding the door open.

"Congratulations." He nods as I try to slide into my seat with grace despite the size of the dress and, like a pro, he folds my train in after me as my father jumps in the other side.

"This is amazing." I look around in awe at the luxurious interior of a car stocked for fun because there are buckets of iced champagne nestling on brackets and some crystal glasses waiting to be used. A small white box is handed to me by my father tied in a pink satin bow and he says softly, "From Marcus."

"Really." My heart is hammering as I open the box and as I remove the solid silver heart from the padding inside, I blink back tears at the generous gift. It's so beautiful, perfect even, and my father says softly, "He asked me to give this to you. He told me he wanted you to know before you reached the church that he is with you every step of the way."

"He did?"

My fingers shake as I try to fasten it around my neck, and as my father helps, I think about the man who gave it to me. Another sweet thought, a well-placed gesture perhaps to make sure I honour our agreement, but a heart, his heart, possibly. I hope so, anyway.

As we set off the short distance to the church, we are accompanied by soft classical music playing from the speakers that remind me a lot of Marcus. Strong, perfect and so beautiful, it blinds you to anything else. And if I didn't know better, I'd almost believe he loved me back.

∾

A SMALL CROWD has gathered at the church boundary and as my father takes my hand and helps me from the car, a cheer goes up and I hear, "She looks so beautiful... a princess... she's so lucky... I wish it was me... look at that dress.... god I hate her."

Smiling, I wave like I'm visiting royalty and hope that last comment was just a jealous one and not really meant.

As I walk beside my father, holding onto his arm, my entire life flashes before my eyes. My past, present and possible future, good and bad, makes me falter a little and my dad says anxiously, "Are you ok, sweetheart?"

I can see Florrie looking concerned as she waits and mentally, I pull up my big girl's pants and make my decision.

I couldn't back out now if I tried because when Sammy Jo Miles makes a decision and a promise, she never breaks it.

So what if my heart will be trampled and burned to ashes, scattered at my feet in a big 'I told you so.' At least I would have had him for two years, some marriages never make it past their first anniversary, so I have that assurance at least. And what a two years it will be, I'll make sure of that, so I smile with a sudden bravery and say with determination, "I'm fine. More than fine."

We reach the door that looks so romantic with its garland of roses and hydrangeas, and does a good job of lifting my spirits. Clutching the silver heart, I dare to dream and my father leans in and whispers, "I'm so proud of you, sweetheart. I always was and always will be. I love you, never forget that."

Fanning my eyes, I blink back the tears and manage to whisper, "I love you too, dad."

This is that moment when a girl becomes a woman. When she leaves the safety of her home and family to step out on her own. The moment when she takes absolute charge of her life and owns her decisions. No one to blame but herself and for the first time, I take strength in that. Sammy Jo has grown up and made up her mind and is walking towards an uncertain future that will only be as good as the hard work she puts into it. Nothing is for granted in this life and you must work at it to reap the rewards like any business. This is what this is, the business of marriage, and maybe Marcus and I stand a greater chance than many at making it work.

To my surprise, a haunting melody beckons us inside and I say in surprise, "Wow, Mrs Judd has been studying hard on YouTube. I thought we were marching in to Onward Christian Soldiers.

My father laughs and whispers, "Marcus arranged for a concert pianist at the last minute. He had to clear it with the church first, but money talks and they were more than happy to oblige."

"He did that, really." Once again, he's surprised me and a warm feeling captures my heart and wraps it in rainbows.

Could this work. Right now, it certainly feels that way and so, with a deep breath, I prepare to meet the man himself.

CHAPTER 34

The cool stone of the church is in direct contrast to the sunshine outside and the sense of occasion it creates makes me hold my breath. I see the beautiful flower arrangements on the window sills and the candles burning brightly beside them. The enchanting melody beckons me inside and as I step through the door, I cling a little tighter to my father's arm.

The first person I see is Jim Burrows, looking dapper in a freshly pressed checked shirt, standing beside a rosy-cheeked woman who I'm guessing is his wife, Trudy. She is dabbing at her eyes with a hanky, and I smile nervously as we pass. I can't even look at the man I am walking towards because it's taking all my self-control just to put one foot in front of the other.

Knowing my own family is sparse, I am surprised to see the church is crowded with guests on both sides. As I look to my left, I stop suddenly and blink because I know that face. In fact, the more I look, the more I recognise and I gasp in shock when I see my uncles, aunts, cousins and friends.

My father chuckles softly beside me and whispers, "Stay focused, princess, keep your eye on the prize."

The tears spill down my cheeks as I stare at their loving smiles, not sure if I'm hallucinating due to the hangover. To my right are many people I don't know, along with some I do. Maria, Miranda and Laura from the Cosy Kettle and Mrs Jenkins beside a man I assume is her husband.

My eye is drawn to the front of the church, where I see Camilla flanked by a solid wall of muscle, and I laugh as she winks as I move past her.

Then my eyes are drawn to only one man and I almost step back at the look powering from his eyes.

It's as if he's reaching out and pulling me in because this man will ruin me. Just the look in his eye, the chiselled features and the fact he is dressed like my vision of heaven, makes me weak at the knees and desperate to be by his side because in this moment of time, that's the only place I want to be.

He overwhelms me in every way. He makes the world remain out of focus with only him in it. He is everything I want in my life, despite the circumstances, although from the look in his eye, he is pulling off an Oscar winning performance.

"LADIES AND GENTLEMEN." I jump as the vicar starts shouting and I think the whole congregation jumps with me.

"Who gives this woman to this man?" Quickly, my dad steps forward and almost pushes me into Marcus's arms. I stumble a little and he reaches out and catches me and as I look up into his eyes, my whole world rights itself.

"I do." My father's voice is husky as he kisses me on the cheek and then moves away and joins my mum and my - brother. I blink in disbelief as Ryan stares at me proudly and then winks as my mouth drops open when I see my grandparents sitting proudly by his side.

It's all too much and I'm overwhelmed. So completely and utterly overwhelmed, I can't help it and sob so loudly it's all you can hear in the church.

I can't appear to stop either and as I am folded into those strong arms and Marcus drops a light kiss on top of my head, I cry the happiest tears of my life.

I take a moment to let the emotion out and only when a hanky appears and I dry my tears, do I look up into the face of the man who has made this all happen and whisper, "Thank you."

He smiles and the love in his eyes shocks me a little as he whispers, "Because I love you."

"You do."

"I do."

"Not yet." The vicar looks slightly worried and says, "We haven't got to that part yet."

Pulling back, he shouts, "WE ARE GATHERED HERE TODAY…"

I can't concentrate on anything he is saying as I hold hands with my husband to be. The man who told me he loved me and backed it up with the sweetest gesture I have ever experienced. As we stare into each other's eyes, I know I made the right decision.

"NOW FOR THE VOWS."

Marcus looks a little nervous as he holds my hand tightly and says in a husky voice.

"Samantha Josephine Hermione Miles." He grins and I giggle as his brothers chuckle behind him.

"I never expected to fall in love – ever. It wasn't for me. I didn't want it and never thought it would happen. Then I met you."

A sigh from the guests ripples around the church like a Mexican wave and I feel a shiver of pleasure at the look in his eyes. "The fact you were dating my three brothers at the time was an inconvenience."

A shocked hush descends on the church and I smile nervously. "I also never expected to fall in love at first sight, but that's exactly what happened when you came for the job interview. Even then I reached for your hand, knowing I never wanted to let you go. I knew I wanted you to be with me forever, but how could I explain that without sounding like a fool?"

He looks behind him and smiles and, in this moment, I see the power of a family such as this. One solid unit that comes together when it counts and I feel proud to be a part of something so amazing.

Turning back, he smiles into my eyes and says loudly. "I'm sorry, Sammy, I tricked you."

The guests shift in their seats as they suspect a twist in the tale, and yet I'm not worried. How can I worry when he is looking at me with such devotion and I nod with encouragement?

"I don't need to marry you to get my inheritance."

A gasp echoes around the church as the congregation learns for the first time the nature of this wedding.

"But I thought…" He shakes his head and winks, and I see the usual cocky player return that makes me weak at the knees.

"When my father made the will, it was to mess with our lives long after his was over. We all made a pact not to let him win. We agreed on what we wanted and were happy to wait as long as it took. When we met you though, we had a different battle on our hands because two of us were interested in the same girl."

I look at Dom, who smiles and shrugs and Marcus turns and says to his brother, "I'm sorry, Dom, I couldn't let that happen, so I made Sammy an offer she couldn't refuse. I knew you had the same thing in mind and so I got there first. It was the truth in a way, and for a moment there, I thought dad had won. Messed with our minds and set us against one another and I'm sorry for my part in that."

Turning to me, he says with a slight break to his voice. "I would have done anything to make you mine, Sammy Jo. Even go against my family because I wanted you so badly. But this is your choice to make now you have all the facts."

Suddenly, he drops to his knee, and a hush falls on the church as he says loudly, "Will you marry me, Sammy Jo, and for real this time, forever and make me the happiest man alive?"

Just seeing him on his knees declaring his undying love for me is like a fairy-tale. I can almost taste the tension in the air as time stops for a moment to appreciate the drama and with the biggest smile on my face, I nod vigorously, "Of course I will. I love you."

The congregation cheers as Marcus stands and pulls me in for a kiss and yet before our lips connect, we hear a loud, "DO YOU, Marcus Sheridan Hudson, take Samantha Josephine Hermione Miles to be your wedded wife, to live together in marriage? Do you promise to love her, comfort her, honour and keep her for better or worse, for richer or poorer, in sickness and health, and forsaking all others, be faithful only to her, for as long as you both shall live?"

He holds my hands to his lips and kisses them gently before saying loudly, "I do."

"DO YOU, Samantha Josephine Hermione Miles, take Marcus Sheridan Hudson to be your wedded husband to live together in marriage? Do you promise to love him, comfort him, honour and keep him for better or worse, for richer or poorer, in sickness and health and forsaking all others, be faithful only to him so long as you both shall live?"

I feel the tears building once again as I say just as loud, "I do."

Because I do love him and what surprises me the most is that he loves me too.

The rest of the service goes by without a hitch and as Marcus slides the ring on my finger, my eyes water as the significance hits me. Two people are now one. It seems crazy to think of the circumstances that brought us to this point, but fate works in mysterious ways and it wouldn't surprise me if fate was Marcus's middle name because he is the most mysterious man I think I've ever met.

Seeing the ring that binds us together reminds me how little input I've had in this wedding, but then again, I wouldn't change a thing. Every moment is a delicious surprise, crafted with sweet thoughts and love.

I do love him; I wasn't lying about that, and I love his family and Dream Valley. I'm looking forward to my life here – with him and as the vicar says the words I have waiting for, "I NOW PRONOUNCE YOU HUSBAND AND WIFE. YOU MAY NOW KISS THE BRIDE."

My heart goes into free-fall.

Just the look in my husband's eyes takes my breath away as they sparkle with pure love – for me.

Stepping forward the short distance, he runs his hand around my waist and tugs me gently towards him, his other hand wrapping around the back of my head to hold it in place and as our lips touch gently, it makes my heart flutter because this time it feels different.

He loves me. He declared it before everyone we know and the fact he deepens the kiss and shows me just how much, makes me wish this moment would never end.

CHAPTER 35

We make our way outside after the most beautiful experience of my life. From the soft classical music, to the flowers and candles. The choir that sounded like angels and the soloist who sang a beautiful rendition of Ave Maria as we signed the registers. I was certainly feeling the love as it filled the church and cemented our decision. This was always meant to be and the fact Marcus fell in love at first sight didn't sound ridiculous at all because I did too.

Marcus grasps my hand tightly, and as we pose for the camera and share many more kisses, my heart dances with happiness and every doubt in my mind has disappeared in a puff of happily ever after.

Family and friends crowd out from the church and we are swamped with happiness as they take it in turn to offer their congratulations.

It feels weird introducing Marcus to my family for the very first time. I'm surprised to learn that there was no stag do last night. Instead, they had been arranging this whole surprise. Coaches were dispatched to transport my family and train tickets arranged. This morning, bright and early, they were ferrying guests from the station and nearby hotels and I can't believe they pulled it off.

"Sammy, my baby, I am so proud."

The familiar tones of my grandmother reach me and I step into her arms with a tear and a smile. It feels good to see them and as we cling together, I am so grateful they made it.

"You certainly know how to throw a surprise."

My Grandpa laughs loudly beside me and I turn and draw him into the hug. They are my only two grandparents still living because my father's parents died a few years ago, just one year apart.

"Thanks for coming."

I whisper emotionally and my nan whispers back, "I'm so happy we made it. I can't believe you were going to marry without us. I still can't quite wrap my head around that."

"Leave her alone, Willy. Sammy can do whatever she likes."

Grinning, I look at my grandmother, Willy (short for Wilhelmina) fondly. "You will stay for a while, won't you?"

I'm keen to catch up with them and my grandfather says gently, "We will stay until we go off."

"What does that even mean?" Laughing, they both say together, "Guests are like fish. They go off after three days."

"Benjamin Franklin, I believe." A hand wraps around my waist and Marcus joins us, and my grandfather nods with approval. "You're right."

Marcus grins. "That wouldn't bother us, would it, darling? You can stay as long as you like."

It feels so weird to be standing here with my husband and my grandparents. I don't think I've had enough time to mentally prepare for that image and I'm still wrapping my own head around it but I wouldn't change a thing because it feels nice, right and as if we were always going to end up here.

The photographs seem to take forever and it makes me smile when Camilla takes her place beside Marcus and her three strippers stand behind her. I don't think I'll ever stop laughing about that and love the fact her sons don't seem to care and just chat with them like old friends.

My brother already seems familiar with them and I heard it's because he arrived last night and helped organise everything. I manage to grab a private moment with him, and he rolls his eyes. "Trust you, Sammy, you don't do things the easy way."

"Do you like him, Ryan?" I feel so anxious about that because I want my family to love Marcus as much, ok maybe not as much, as I do.

"He seems a great guy, Sammy. A little intense sometimes, but I'm sure you'll soften his edges over time."

"I love that he's intense, it's exciting."

He pulls a face. "I don't want to know. So, Dream Valley, it seems a good enough place to set up home. Does this mean we won't be seeing much of you?"

"Of course not." Lowering my voice, I whisper, "I think there may be a few new houses springing up soon, perhaps you should put your name down for one of them, mum and dad too."

Ryan looks around him and I see him watching Maria and he grins. "I may look into that."

This time I roll my eyes because Ryan could give Marcus and his brothers a run for their money when it comes to the ladies and whoever grabs this man's wedding finger will be a very lucky one indeed.

∾

The limousine is waiting and I'm looking forward to being alone with Marcus because it feels like a lifetime ago since we were.

As mum folds my train into the car, he slides in beside me and it feels good to close the door on the madness and take a moment to breathe.

Luckily, Jim's not driving and we are soon on our way and yet the driver doesn't take the turning left towards Valley House, where a marquee has been set up on the grounds.

"Where are we going?"

Marcus pulls my face to his and whispers, "We're going to lose ourselves while the guests make their way to the reception."

Oh." I stare into his eyes and he whispers, "Thank you."

His lips touch mine and I welcome the kiss because finally we are alone. The glass partition separates us from the driver and we have some time apart from the madness to enjoy this moment.

Marcus kisses me with a passion that gets my heart racing because I have wanted this kiss since the day I met him on the cruise. One with meaning behind it. A lover's kiss. The kiss that settles my heart and allows me to stop pretending. Not that I ever was and, so it appears, neither was he.

He pulls back and says huskily, "I thought I had two years to make you fall in love with me. That was my reason for lying to you. To make you stay and when Dom told me he was going to do the same, I lost my mind."

It feels strange thinking of the two brothers fighting over me behind my back, and I remember how much fun I had with Dom on the cruise. He was paired up with me one evening on the cruising in love programme and it was a fun night. Marcus wasn't even on the programme, which surprises me because his other three brothers were.

"Why weren't you involved with Cruising in Love, I never really understood why?"

He strokes my face gently and stares into my eyes. "Because I wasn't looking for anyone. I don't like messing around and couldn't think of anything worse. I'm not my brothers, Sammy and I'm not my father."

Thinking about Maria, I'm not so sure, but how can I raise that subject on my wedding day? I don't need to worry though because Marcus says gruffly, "If you must know, I was feeling bad. I'm ashamed to admit I had a one-night stand with Maria the night before the cruise."

He looks at me anxiously, but I nod. "I know, she told me."

I feel him tense as he groans. "I deserved that because I'm not proud of my reaction. I don't do one-night stands - ever. I'm not even sure why I did that night, but one thing led to another and we ended up back at her flat. I regretted it almost immediately and felt so bad I left when she was asleep. I felt as if I'd let myself down and her because I have tried so hard to be different from my father. The trouble is, in fighting so hard, I've denied myself the freedom many guys enjoy. I don't date, I don't sleep around and can count on the fingers of one hand the number of women I've dated.

Now I'm thinking about perfect elastic tie woman and I feel bad for saying, "Tell me about them."

He looks surprised. "You really want to know on your wedding day."

Looking down, I say in a small voice, "Maybe because I have never really felt good enough for you, Marcus. In my mind you have dated a string of glamorous women and I don't measure up."

He pulls my face to his and smiles. "You are the only one I wanted to marry. The only one I can't stop thinking about and the only one I want to spend the rest of my life with. You are THE one."

Then he kisses me again and I couldn't care less about his past girlfriends. What difference does it make now? We all have a past and I'm happy to leave ours where they belong – behind us.

The rest of the journey is spent sipping champagne wrapped in each other's arms. Stealing kisses and sharing loaded looks that make my heart beat furiously as I imagine my life with this man.

When we finally crawl up the driveway to Valley House to begin our married life together, I finally feel as if I'm coming home.

CHAPTER 36

I never thought I'd be a guest at my own wedding, but that's exactly what it felt like. Everything has been planned meticulously. The floral arrangements, the amazing food, the beautifully decorated marquee, and the concert pianist who serenaded us throughout. Marcus was a little worried, but I loved every minute of it. The fact it was all a surprise made it feel more magical somehow. Apparently, Camilla and Marcus planned the whole thing between them. He was so anxious to make it a dream wedding, he just hoped the bride showed up.

Love at first sight is now my favourite kind of love because it has delivered everything to me on a platter and most of all, I am married to the most amazing man – one I never thought would feel the same way about me in a million years.

Nothing was left to chance and as the darkness falls and we sway to the music wrapped in each other's arms, I am now a firm believer in fairy tales.

"Are you happy?" Marcus nuzzles my neck and I shiver with pleasure. "I am."

His hold tightens as he whispers, "I still can't believe this is happening; that you feel the same."

"Same."

Leaning back, I look up at him and love the way his lips instinctively find mine in a long, lingering kiss.

I see Camilla dancing with one of the strippers and laugh to myself when I notice Ryan whisking Maria around the dance floor. Mum and dad are gently swaying to the music and nan and grandpa are looking exhausted as they watch the dancing with interest.

Seeing Jake and Florrie smooching like teenagers, I wonder if we'll be attending another wedding in the near future.

Feeling a tap on my shoulder, I look up in surprise as Dom says, "My turn."

Marcus looks daggers at him and then they both laugh and Marcus says firmly, "One dance, I owe you that at least."

He kisses me sweetly before disappearing over to join my grandparents, leaving me feeling slightly nervous in his brother's arms.

"It all ended well then." Dom smiles as we spin around the dance floor.

"It did."

"I'm happy for you both." His smile relaxes me and I whisper, "Thank you. I'm sorry…"

"No need, Sammy. It was obvious you were meant to be together. Marcus became a different person around you, and I saw your expression when you looked at him. We had fun, but that was it. Now it's as friends, which is a good relationship to have with your sister-in-law."

"I suppose it is." Feeling a lot happier, I see Marcus draw Maria aside as she leaves the dance floor as Ryan joins our grandparents.

Dom follows my eyes and laughs softly. "I'm guessing

that's an awkward conversation. I'd love to watch him squirm."

"She'll be ok. I think the apology will be welcome though. You know, Dom, I still don't believe Marcus hasn't had many girlfriends, it doesn't seem right."

"He had a few but you're right, nowhere near Brad's tally, that man's a machine."

We laugh as Brad leads a giggling local girl out of the marquee and Dom laughs. "He'll never change."

"Maybe he'll meet someone who tests him, possibly doesn't fall for his charms and gives him a reality check."

"I'd like to see that."

We share a grin and he says thoughtfully, "You're good for Marcus, Sammy. He's lighter around you, less introverted, and lets himself go a little. Take the camping trip, for instance. He wouldn't be seen dead in Brad's dogging wagon under normal circumstances, but he did it to make you happy. To make your dream come true."

Laughing, I lower my voice. "Don't tell anyone, but I hate camping. It was more a nightmare of mine than a dream. But keep it to yourself because it was a really sweet thing to do."

Dom throws his head back and laughs loudly, which takes me back to the evening I spent with him on the cruise. We had so much fun, too much really, and I'm happy that he's now my brother-in-law.

"So, one down, three to go, two if you discount Jake."

"Then you'll be waiting a long time because it's doubtful Brad will ever change and I'm in no hurry. I'm all about the business now and it would take someone very special to distract me from that."

"Maybe it will be your mother then."

Dom looks disgusted at the thought, and it doesn't help that Camilla is pressed between two strippers as they gyrate against her on the dance floor.

"She'll be ok." Dom's voice softens as he regards his mother behaving badly. "She's had a lot to put up with over the years and deserves to let her hair down. I hope she does meet someone else, someone kind, loving, and treats her with respect. Older than those guys though - much older." He shivers, making me laugh and as the music stops, he says gallantly, "As your husband is chatting in the corner with a past special friend, allow me to escort you to the bar."

Watching Marcus explaining himself makes me love him even harder because Maria deserves every bit of grovelling he is no doubt doing over there.

I link arms with Dom and we head to the bar where we join Jake and Florrie, who are doing shots of tequila and taking selfies.

"Sammy." She throws her arms around me and slurs, "Thank god one of us actually made it through a wedding, I'll drink to that."

Jake grins. "Maybe we've had too much. I want you conscious for the finale of the evening."

"Jake, I'm shocked." Florrie giggles as he rolls his eyes and says, "Fireworks. I think they're about to start."

Florrie looks ecstatic because she's always loved a big bang and I'm no different, so we head outside along with the last remaining guests and gather in the slightly damp field a little way from the marquee.

Marcus soon joins me and pulls me close to his side, wrapping his jacket around my shoulders and kissing me sweetly. "I hope you like fireworks. It was mum's idea. She wanted one of those full-on laser shows with Disney music, but I persuaded her to settle for a five minute display with classical music instead."

"Spoilsport." Giggling, I snuggle into his arms as the show begins and as the sky lights up with all the colours of the rainbow, it seems fitting that Marcus's choice of his favourite classical tunes serenades us.

The perfect end to the perfect day and I couldn't have wished for more.

I have it all, at least I think I do, and I'm looking forward to my life in Dream Valley.

EPILOGUE

FIVE MONTHS LATER

The view takes my breath away. It always has and as I stand holding Marcus's hand, I still can't believe I'm here at all.

"So, your dream has finally come true."

I smile up at my husband as he grips my hand a little tighter and I see the pride in his eyes.

"I have everything I ever wanted."

Leaning down, he kisses me softly and my heart lifts as we share a moment that feels as if it's been a long time coming.

This morning we received the planning approval for Dream Valley Heights and are on our way to celebrate with the rest of the family at The Olive Tree.

But first we came here, to where it all began and as I shiver against the slightly frosty air, I love that Marcus pulls me close and tucks me into his side where I always feel happiest.

The past few months have been spent settling in and preparing for this day. First came the inheritance, then the endless meetings with the planning department, headed up by the ferocious Elspeth Grainger.

It was all worth it though because now we have a plan and a date for the work to start. February the 20th when the diggers will roll in and change this landscape forever.

It still feels wrong on every level and I sigh, the tears biting behind my eyes as I contemplate this story changing.

Marcus squeezes me tighter and whispers, "The animals will be ok. I'll build them a mansion if that's what you want."

A small smile tugs at the corner of my mouth as I imagine them curled up in their burrows waiting out winter, and it's a horrible thought ruining all of that for bricks and mortar.

Luckily, the area of land most suited to wildlife has been ring fenced as a nature reserve and Marcus has arranged for specialist help to move the animals before building work starts. That was my number one priority, even if it wasn't his and, like the amazing man he is, he made sure I was happy first.

In fact, he hasn't put a foot wrong since we married on the best day of my life. It has been the best time getting to one another and, if anything, we are more in love now than on our wedding day. Isn't that what's supposed to happen? Marriage is just the beginning and the ties strengthen and love deepens with every year that passes. It's hard to imagine loving him any more than I do already and I make sure to take a selfie of us to put in my memory box. This place is special for many reasons and I'm guessing when people start moving in to the homes we create, they will also share special memories of a place that was previously out of bounds.

In developing the land, we are giving many people a chance to settle in a magical place and create their own happily ever after.

We will continue to live at Valley House as a family for as

long as they want to. Camilla, I know, already has renovations underway in the Lodge House on the edge of the estate and her Pinterest boards are exploding with ideas. Jake and Florrie are enjoying getting to one another still and are in no hurry to tie the knot. Her beauty business is doing well and his computer game is the fastest selling one this side of Christmas.

As for Brad, he will never change, it seems, and it's a rare sight to see his dogging wagon parked in the driveway at night. He's a lovable rogue, who can do no wrong in his mother's eyes, and I expect he will be the last one to leave.

Dom is busy with the business as he tries to prove he's better than his father ever was, and I just love spending my days and nights with Marcus, planning our future and making it count.

The ice twists my toes in its unforgiving grasp and the wind whips against my face, my breath providing the only heat and Marcus says gruffly, "We should go and meet the others, it's a shame though."

"Why?" I shiver as he pulls me against him and stares deep into my eyes. "Because I just want to celebrate with you."

As he dips his head and claims my lips, I share his need. There is never a time that I don't physically ache for Marcus Hudson and I hope that never changes.

As we finally make it to the car, a more practical BMW SUV, I remember the little red sports with a fond memory. I finally asked about elastic tie woman and at first Marcus was a little confused. Then he started to laugh as he told me the tie was his. He had longer hair before the cruise and used the elastic to secure it when he had the roof down. I remember he showed me a photograph of him with hair touching the base of his neck and I was surprised at how much it suited him. He looked like a rock star and he always will be in my eyes.

Marcus turns on the engine and the heated seats soon kick in and I'm grateful when the temperature increases to less critical levels in my frozen body.

As we speed down the hill accompanied by the usual classical music, we pass the sweet little church that has become so dear to us both. Seeing the Christmas tree standing proudly outside, resting against the door, I feel a shiver of pleasure as I anticipate spending my first Christmas in Dream Valley.

Almost as if he can read my mind, Marcus laughs softly.

"It will be an interesting Christmas this year. Have you heard, Reverend Bowers has relocated?"

"No." I stare at him in shock. "Since when?"

"Last week. It all happened so suddenly. He was needed in another parish, a larger one, and they are sending a military vicar to take his place."

"That sounds – scary, actually."

I feel a wave of disappointment because I have grown extremely fond of the rather pompous vicar with his church rules, and Marcus nods. "I'm sure it will annoy a few of the villagers. They don't like change and never have."

"When does he arrive?"

"Tomorrow, I think. He's got a lot to deal with though, it's a busy time for the church, the busiest time of the year and I suppose that's why Reverend Bowers was needed in the bigger town."

"Well, I'm sure he can rely on the locals to help, your mother for one."

Camilla Hudson heads up every committee going in Dream Valley and I'm sure will be the first in line to greet him.

Just thinking about experiencing Christmas in Dream Valley makes me smile. Our first one together and my first married one. It will be the calm before the storm and I'm looking forward to making many memories, revisiting old traditions and inventing a few myself. Decorating the tree and gathering sprigs of holly and mistletoe to hang around Valley House. Shopping in Riverton and enjoying mugs of steaming hot chocolate by an open fire and hunting for the perfect Christmas tree to decorate.

Yes, this will be a perfect Christmas and like a child eagerly anticipating it, I am counting down the days in my mind and preparing for the most amazing Christmas ever.

∼

Thank you for reading.
I hope you enjoyed this story and are interested to learn what happens next.
Christmas in Dream Valley is only a click away when we meet the newest addition to the community, The very military Reverend Macmillan and his family.

Surround yourself in all things Christmas and enjoy watching Brad Hudson struggle with his feelings when he meets the very sweet, very prim and proper Vicar's daughter. Can a rogue change on the sniff of a mince pie or will the magic of Christmas fail this time?
Check it out here.

Christmas in Dream Valley

S J Crabb

If you missed Cruising in Love where Sammy Jo and Florrie meet the Hudson brothers you can check it out here.
Cruising in Love

After a happy ever disaster Florence heads off on her honeymoon cruise with her bridesmaid.

Hoping to enjoy two weeks of relaxation on an all-expenses-paid trip of a lifetime she was hoping to recharge and reflect on the cruel blow fate dealt her.

Her bridesmaid has other ideas and before she knows it, they are signed up to the ship's cruising in love programme where single passengers were paired up in a bid to find their shipmate.

Seven dates in seven days with a love match at the end and another week to get to know one another.

Will it be love at first sight or an endless round of disastrous dates with nowhere to hide?

A light-hearted romance about starting again and discovering that everything happens for a very good reason.

~

THANK you for reading Coming Home to Dream Valley.

If you liked it, I would love if you could leave me a review, as I must do all my own advertising.

This is the best way to encourage new readers and I appreciate every review I can get. Please also recommend it to your friends as word of mouth is the best form of advertising. It won't take longer than two minutes of your time, as you only need write one sentence if you want to.

Have you checked out my website? Subscribe to keep updated with any offers or new releases.

sjcrabb.com

WHEN YOU VISIT MY WEBSITE, you may be surprised because I don't just write Romantic comedy.

I also write under the pen names M J Hardy & Harper Adams. I send out a monthly newsletter with details of all my releases and any special offers but aside from that, you don't hear from me very often.

If you like social media, please follow me on mine where I am a lot more active and will always answer you if you reach out to me.

Why not take a look and see for yourself and read Lily's Lockdown, a little scene I wrote to remember the madness when the world stopped and took a deep breath?

LILY'S LOCKDOWN

More books by S J Crabb

<u>The Diary of Madison Brown</u>
My Perfect Life at Cornish Cottage
My Christmas Boyfriend
Jetsetters
More from Life
A Special Kind of Advent
Fooling in love
Will You
Holly Island
Aunt Daisy's Letter
The Wedding at the Castle of Dreams
My Christmas Romance
Escape to Happy Ever After
Cruising in Love
Coming Home to Dream Valley
Christmas in Dream Valley

sjcrabb.com

KEEP IN TOUCH

You can also follow me on social media below.

Facebook

Instagram

Twitter

Website

Bookbub

Amazon

Printed in Great Britain
by Amazon